# THE CONSORT

# THE CONSORT

## J. WARREN

Queer Space
New Orleans

Published in the United States of America by
Queer Space
A Rebel Satori Imprint
www.rebelsatoripress.com

Paperback ISBN: 978-1-60864-235-9
Ebook ISBN: 978-1-60864-236-6

# CONTENTS

# THE CONSORT

# ARRIVAL

Arriving at Ganymede station for the connecting flight out of the solar system has always been a giant pain in the ass. No one goes there except to catch the outbound superfast crates, so they don't bother making the place look nice for the locals because there aren't any locals. Just us transients who are only in the station long enough to take the train from the A gates over to the C gates and maybe hook up in one of the bathrooms one last time before going into the freezers. Just in case the cool down process winds up damaging something, you know?

It's happened more than once out here.

The most difficult part for me has always been the smell. I mean, it's not like the place smells horrible, but it is an under-ventilated hub with thousands of people moving through it practically ever hour on the hour. It's not exactly the Spring Gardens, you know?

Still, I've smelled worse.

I'm doing that thing we all do, here, and wandering through the gift shop. Staring at candies I don't want to eat before the big freeze, at Martian beers that would probably be good any other time, but, again, the freezers. It's not dangerous, per se, to eat or drink before they plug you in for the long ride out, but I've never done it and I'm not about to change my routine now.

A tall platinum blonde is looking me up and down. I can't tell if maybe he just likes what he sees and wants to get in a little alone time before heading to Hansen's World or Beakman 453B or wherever, or if he's actually recognized me. Maybe a bit of both.

I mean, I don't try to disguise myself, really. Especially not out here. What would be the point?

I can see him working himself up enough courage to come over. I look at my watch. If we're going to do this, it needs to be sooner rather than later. This time I'm going farther than I've ever gone before. The ship is so big it can't actually dock—I have to catch a shuttle out to it.

I turn to him just in time for him to say, "Excuse me, I don't mean to be rude, but aren't you—?"

I smile the official smile from the front of the vids. His accent is pure Martian, which is cute. I kind of have a thing for Martian boys.

"Oh, man, I knew it! None of my friends will believe me. Can I get your—," he trails off, holding his PAD out to me.

"Actually," I say, "I was wondering if maybe you wanted to go somewhere a little more private?"

He blushes and looks around. That's a yes.


"Mister Van Ryan?" the woman asks. I nod. She gestures to her left. "This way, please."

I follow her down an empty corridor away from the line of other people. I've been in that other line before. They'll be herded into a bay with freezers and given instructions by impatient crew. Treated like cargo more than anything else.

"Here you are," the woman says. The nametag on her jumpsuit reads Okonkwo. She's gesturing again, and I can't help but notice her immaculate manicure. She's indicating an empty room. I sit down on the leather couch. The room has been made to look like pictures I've seen of train compartments from the 1800s. There's even a faux wood blind hanging over the window to my right.

"Champagne?" she asks.

"No, thank you," I say.

"Welcome aboard," she says. "My name is Aidy. If you'd like to remove your clothes now, I'll bring you a sleepsuit and some slippers and then we'll get you tucked in." Her smile seems almost genuine. That's how good she is.

She's giving me privacy to change clothes. I don't tell her that it's unnecessary. There is no part of my body that hasn't been photographed, 3- and 4-D modeled, digitized and rendered, etc. At this point in my life, my body qualifies as a tourist attraction.

Back down that hall in the economy freezers, the others are being commanded to strip and given a pair of briefs (if they have identified as male on their ticket), or a pair of briefs and a sports bra (if they have identified as female). The technician who will be coming along to them each in turn in a few moments will jam the needles in with little thought for their comfort and likely won't even address them. The idea is to get them prepped and chilled down quickly before any of them can protest the way they are being treated.

Aidy comes back and hands me a sleepsuit. I've only ever heard about these, never seen one before. It slides on and immediately I'm warm in all the right places. It has little ports for the IVs. She also hands me slippers. They're more comfortable than anything I've ever worn on my feet before in my life. I might be imagining it, but I could swear they conform to my arches immediately.

"Right this way," Aidy says, gesturing with her impeccable nails again.

I could get used to this.

I notice as we leave for the next compartment that someone comes

3

in and picks up my clothes. Aidy doesn't even have to do it.

The next compartment has a polished glass and steel tube in it. Everything sparkles and feels immaculate. The second we enter the glass slides open and the bank of screens nearby light up. I can't help but notice, too, that this tube is twice as wide as the ones I've been in before. The ones back down the hallway.

"Please don't worry about a thing—your clothes and personal belongings are being stored in the room through that door," she says, gesturing to the door opposite the one we've just come through. "They are perfectly safe. If you would please enter your capsule, we can get started tucking you in." I hear it, now. She's been trained to say these exact phrases. I don't mind.

I climb up onto the cushion that is more comfortable than my bed at home.

"Of course I do apologize but you'll feel two small pinches. If you would like, I can count down to them?"

"No, that's alright," I say. She nods. I feel the pinches on my arm. It turns out, though, that Thomas was right; the people down the hall, they are feeling thick, cold sludgy syrup pour into their veins. I'm not feeling anything except the sudden drowsiness.

"There you are," Aidy says. "I'll be the face you see when you wake up, so don't worry. You're perfectly safe." I'm starting to doze. Her face grows blurry. "As always, we want to thank you for choosing us as your long distance carrier. We know that you have choices—," at that point there is only blackness.

Choices, I think before drifting off. Wouldn't that have been nice.

Cold.

"—ster Van Ryan?" From far away I hear sounds. I know I'm supposed to go toward them, but I'm wondering, why bother? I can hear my own breathing but it sounds like it's coming from something else. Some enormous beast out there in the deep darkness surrounding me.

Even that, frightening as it is, makes me think maybe being eaten alive isn't such a bad way to go.

"Mister Van Ryan? Can you hear me?" I hear again.

Oh. Right. The world.

"Mister Van Ryan, it's me Aidy. Don't worry. When you open your eyes it'll still be very dark. We are going to bring the lights up gradually so as not to shock your system. I just wanted to let you know that we are beginning our deceleration now. You've slept the whole way and we're very close to arriving at our destination. You are perfectly safe."

I wasn't worried, but it's nice to know.

"As you come out of sleep it is normal to experience vertigo. Some passengers also report extremes of hunger. You'll need to visit the bathroom which will be immediately forward of the capsule. Don't worry, there will be arrows on the floor directing you. I'm going to step out so you can have a bit of privacy, but if at any point you feel you need assistance, please don't hesitate to call for me using the red button on the bracelet that I'm placing on your arm now."

Far off in some other country there is a slight pressure. I think that place used to be called my wrist, but who can be certain?

An hour later? A day? A thousand years? I open my eyes. The room has just enough light that I can see the walls. I sit up on my elbows. Three seconds too late I remember that there are tubes still connected to me and panic for just a moment that I may have just pulled some of them out. I look down to find that they are no longer connected. On my wrist is a clear plastic bracelet, just as Aidy had said there would be. There is a red button on it. Next to the button it says, Van Ryan, J.

5

Before I remember, I think, that's not my name.

"Ah," Aidy says when she comes back in, "you're awake."

I try to smile at her. My face mostly works.

I see her take her hand away from the red button. People over time have come to call it the panic button. I don't know that it ever had a real name other than that. It's the button she can push in case of a passenger waking up in a delirious panic attack. A pilot I once knew told me to always look for that button as I come out of the freezer. It's important to see the attendant take their hand away from it.

This is a bit different, though; I'm already away from the freezer. They've moved me to the special "warm room" that they advertise as a premium for their top tier guests (because when you are paying as much as it costs to be first class on a liner going out this deep, they don't just call you a "passenger" anymore). I notice, too, that I'm in their premium white pajamas with their corporate logo stitched in silver on the right breast pocket. I've been cleaned of all the freezer fluid and someone has even applied balm to my lips. All of this was in the brochure, mind, but I wasn't at all certain what was going to happen all the way out here on this end of things.

"Now that you're awake, we will be adjusting your balances," Aidy says. She presses a button next to the bed and a small tray slides from the wall. It has a small beige rectangle and two tiny glass containers. One has an amber liquid in it, the other a cloudy grayish-white. She slides one on to the top of the rectangle and presses it against my arm. I feel a tiny, sharp pain that goes away almost instantly. She does the same with the other. On the screen next to her, a display of a skull, presumably mine, went from a yellow to green. "There," Aidy says with satisfaction. It almost makes me happy to make her happy with the change in readout.

"If you'll try to sit up for me," she says. As I do, my body moving sluggishly, she rests her hand at the base of my skull. I wait for the wave of nausea but it doesn't come. Again, the premium drugs they use are fantastic. "I'll step out, now. To your right is a shower if you'd like to use it, though you've already been cleaned and moisturized. Some guests like to use it to get their circulation going. The clothes that you gave us to have ready for you upon awakening are there, as well. There are a full range of complimentary cosmetics available for you to use in your gift bag, which is also already located on the counter. Once you're done, simply step through the gray door and I'll be waiting on the other side to escort you to your shuttle."

Once she's gone, I swing my legs over the side of the table and slide my full weight onto them. No rubberiness or shake at all. I smile to myself. I want a quick, almost scalding shower to get reacquainted with my body. She was right, I already feel clean, but it'll be nice to do a quick check of everything. The heat is glorious. Their complimentary cosmetics are all from a line that is incredibly expensive back on Earth. Though I don't really need it, I give my face a nice shave and a rubdown with lotion. The mirror shows the face I expect to see, finally. I slide into the clothes I had left for myself, correctly guessing that I'd want semi-casual. A little bit of comfort but still presentable.

The message I had gotten said that one of the staff, not the man himself, would be picking me up from the shuttleport. At the time I had been able to put off any nervousness by saying that it was a long time before I had to worry about what he was like or what he would think of me. Those butterflies were back, though, now that he was just a shuttle ride below me.

"Mr. Van Ryan?" Aidy says as I come around the corner. Once I finish dressing a computer tells me to follow the lighted arrows to disembark. Aidy's waiting at the other end. She hands me a PAD. "On behalf of the company, let me say thank you for choosing us for your long distance travel. Here is a complimentary pad with information about Elgram 34c already cued up. You'll also find a complimentary subscription to the newsfeed so that you can catch up on local events on your ride down in the shuttle. Finally, there is also a complimentary scan readout of all your vitals during the trip for you to take to whichever local doctor you choose so that they can begin a file for you."

"Thank you," I say, more than a little overwhelmed.

"If you'll just stare at the red dot with a relaxed face for a moment," she says. On the screen of the PAD is a little red dot with a white X in the middle. I stare at it for a second and then there is a sound like a wind chime in a breeze. The screen says Thank You! and then fades to the company's logo and a few data markers.

"Right through this door," Aidy says, "is the shuttle. Your seat is reserved and that seat number will come through on the pad as soon as you step on board. Please take your seat, buckle in, and prepare for entry. Is there anything else I can do for you today?" It's only just then, in that tiny little moment, that I see it in the way the light bounces off the skin on her face: Aidy is an android. A particularly advanced model, too, because it has taken me this long to get it. I wonder if I still need to be polite.

"Thank you," I say. I figure politeness exchanges are probably the triggers for the program to move forward. She smiles and I wonder why it wasn't more obvious—no one has teeth that perfect or eyes that beautiful. The door behind her irises open.

Just as she said, as soon as I step through the portal, the screen lights up with a number and a letter. Three steps down a bare metal tube I can see another open door. Just inside it, another woman, this one in a protective suit, floats. She gestures for me to come toward her. With each step I take in that direction the gravity disappears until I'm floating, too.

"Mr. Van Ryan?" the woman asks. Her accent is thick. Her name tag reads Barnes. I smile. "Welcome aboard. Your seat is just over here." She gestures to the deck behind her. There are only four seats, over-stuffed, and each with its own window. "Let's get you strapped in for entry." As she moves around me adjusting the straps and buckling the buckles, she asks, "how was your flight?"

"I don't remember a thing," I say.

"Good," she says. "That's our goal. As we expected, we've arrived on time. The time and date on the pad is correct local. Our drop time today will be approximately 30 minutes. We should be wheels on deck just before lunch. Pilot says that our approach will be clear as a bell to-day, so you're in for some spectacular views." In the distance I can hear Aidy talking to someone else. Barnes checks the last strap, smiles at me, then turns to go greet the other passengers.

This is the first class shuttle. There were three of us. The other two are much older businessman types. Moustaches, pudge. Not one of my favorite flavors, but I like them because they tend to be grateful for a fuck. Wives stopped finding them attractive after the second kid, you know what I mean? They immediately get lost in their PADs. I can only imagine what kind of business brings them out this far. Then I think about what it is that has brought me this far, and I stop staring. Out the window, the planet is vast stretches of blue dotted with white.

"Mister Van Ryan?" the young woman whose name I've forgotten says as she passes by. "We should be starting our final approach soon. You might want to find a good stopping place," she says, gesturing toward my PAD. She thinks I was reading a book. If only I was that kind of man.

Once we're down through the thick upper atmosphere, and done being bounced around, the flight smooths out. Out the window are miles and miles and miles of ocean. We're near the equator, and the oceans here are calm. The shuttle is still going too fast for me to see any of the life below, but I wonder what kinds of things are under those waves.

"Hello, everyone, this is your pilot speaking," the pleasant voice says over the speaker. I can tell he's worked a long time to get that silky quality into his words. All pilots do. "On behalf of the company, I'd like to thank you again for choosing us for your long distance travel. We know you have a choice in long haul carriers and we appreciate you riding with us. We're about ten minutes out from Velarius station where we will touch down. From there you'll catch your various submersibles to your final destination. We've lucked out today and not only is the air calm, but the seas are, as well. Should be a quiet glide on in. Ensign Barnes is going to be coming through the cabin taking care of any final needs you might have, so sit back, relax, and we'll have you on the deck shortly."

"Is there anything I can get for you?" Barnes (that was her name, I chide myself—I used to be better at that kind of thing) asks. "Hot towel, maybe, to wake up with?"

"Is there coffee?" I ask.

"You bet. I'll be right back," she says. I can feel the shuttle pull as it starts to slow down.

I catch one of the business guys staring at me out of the side of his eye. If I wasn't so worked up over what comes next I'd consider it. Barnes brings me back a cup of coffee and all the various powders that go with it. I've never really liked anything covering up the taste of the beans, so I send them all back with her and sip it straight. It's god awful, but then I can only imagine how long the beans have been sitting in their frozen state. Out the window there is a gleam in the distance. I look out and far off toward the horizon I can see something shining in the sun. A single line of metal against the blue horizon, the gleaming spire of Velarius station on Elgram 34c.

The outermost planet in the outer rim.

My new home.

"Mister Van Ryan?" the voice from the com says.

"Yes?" I ask.

"We'll be beginning our final descent below, now. I know this is your first time at Velarius, so I just wanted to give you a heads up. For new folks, it can be a little...jarring."

"Thank you," I say. I feel like I should do something, but I'm already strapped into the four point harness, and everything is still stowed from when we departed the ship above.

There is a microsecond of panic when the shuttle dips toward the waves and comes down to skim along their surface. We're so low that waves break over the wings. I repeat to myself that this type of craft was designed for this sort of thing. Five minutes later we touch down on the pad and it slowly sinks beneath the waves. I can tell from the sounds of the others in the cabin that they're just as concerned about drowning as I am, but they are keeping it together.

"On behalf of this crew, I would like to take this opportunity to welcome you to Velarius station on Elgram 34c. The local date and time are uploading to your complimentary PAD as we speak, along with data to help you navigate the station below to find the correct submersible to reach your final destination. Again, we thank you for choosing us as your long distance carrier, and hope to see you again soon." I glanced down to see. I pressed the marker on the screen that I swore I wouldn't push and saw the difference between the local date and the date back home. I had already known exactly what the difference would be, but seeing it made the two numbers seem farther apart than they should be. I started to get sad for a moment until I made myself remember that place may have been where I lived for a number of years, but it was never going to be my home. It may have been where lots of my friends lived and where I learned so many things about life, but it wasn't home. I flicked my finger and the pad darkened again.

There was a bump and then a loud sound of the docking clamps rotating and then the shuttle was pulled inside the tower. I looked out the window and just before we were pulled inside I could see the tower extending down and down and down into the abyss of water below. I kept expecting to see lights, even though I knew that the tower was a lone structure, hurled down into the bedrock of the planet by an orbiting ship long ago, and that the settlements were all quite a distance from here.

As soon as the hatch opens, I'm struck by the heat. After being in shuttles and on ships for so long, I'd gotten used to the cold. As the door rolls upward, I felt not only the warmth but I was also the shock of the humidity. My eyes immediately water after having been so dry for so long.

"Mister Van Ryan? This way, please," someone says from below. I look down to see a pristinely dressed woman standing at the bottom of the stairs.

I step down carefully. I've done the embarrassing fall from the walkway thing more than once and I don't care to repeat it.

When I'm at the bottom, I set my bag down and extend my hand to her. She shakes and says, "My name is Venree. I have been asked to escort you to the mansion. If you will please come this way." I reach down for my bag but she says, "You may leave it. Someone will bring it directly." I follow her trying not to let surprise show on my face. I've stayed in some very, very nice places, but none has ever offered to transport my bag directly from shuttle to room.

As we walk side by side, awkwardness creeps in. She is under four foot, so I tower over her. Her stride is the definition of elegance and it makes me pay far too much attention to my own walk.

"His excellency is very excited to meet you. I hope your journey was not too tedious," she says. Her accent is the same as people in old movies, crisp and musical.

"It was fine, thank you. About how long will it take us?"

"Unfortunately, the mansion is quite a distance from this noisy and, frankly, shockingly lacking in security spaceport. There are refreshments in the car if you are hungry or thirsty. You may also nap should you choose—you do not have to stay awake for politeness sake as I am his highness' employee."

I tried to think of some sort of equally polite thing to say in return but couldn't.

Through a winding tangle of corridors we eventually arrive at a doorway in a wall that had seemed otherwise blank. It was only when we stopped that I notice the man who had been following us the whole time. He's huge, and I'm in shock that it's taken me this long to notice him. Venree opens the door and on the other side of it is a set of plush brown leather seats. She gestures for me to step through. I take one and she takes another. The huge man closes the door behind us. When I look back to her, she has her PAD out and has just finished typing instructions. To my left a panel lights up with a delicate blue light, chimes a calming chime, and then I can feel we are moving.

After a second, I can see out the side and front windows and it becomes clear that when she said car, what she meant was a small pod moving through a long tunnel on the outer shell of the station. I catch glimpses of open sea beyond the panes of glass (if it is glass) separating us from tons and tons of water and whatever else is out there.

"I can close the windows down if you would prefer," Venree says.

I want to seem brave to her, so I don't say yes, but some part of me regrets it. What I really need is a drink or a bump of something nice to take the edge off. As if reading my thoughts she opens a bottle of champagne and pours out a glass for me.

"His highness was quite explicit that he wanted you to have a glass of this before arriving. He said that it is your favorite," she says.

I look and, sure enough, it is. A brand that I first found back on Earth when I was young. It is not expensive or particularly well thoughof among wine enthusiasts, but it is one that I developed a taste for when it was all I could afford.

"It must've cost a fortune to get it transported out here," I say. The taste on my tongue immediately brings back memories.

"Yes," Venree says and then goes back to tapping on her PAD.


"Again, I apologize, Mr. Van Ryan," Venree says after a while. "Even for those of us who live here, this is trip can seem…interminable." He gives a weak smile.

After what seems like hours, the car windows go blank again and not long after that the car comes to a stop. The side opens and standing next to it is man as tall as me and dressed in the most exquisitely tailored suit I've ever seen. Venree steps out and waits. I step out and hold my hand out to the man. He shakes it.

"This is Aldous. He is the head butler of the mansion. He will be taking care of your needs for the duration of your stay," Venree says. "It is unlikely you and I will meet again, so I will say good bye to you now." She steps back into the car and the door closes.

"If you will come this way, please," Aldous says. I laugh a bit thinking of how that same sentence has been said to me more in the last few days than in the past several decades. I follow the man through a long series of twisy corridors and we eventually arrive at a single hallway that ends in an elaborate wooden door with a gold knob. He opens it and we step into a very small room. There is a narrow table with a mirror above it and to the right of that, a golden door. The wooden door closes behind us and Aldous pulls a PAD from his pocket. He taps a few commands and I hear massive machinery working for a moment all around us. Then my ears feel the shift in pressure. He has just locked the wooden door and pressurized us.

"For your comfort," he says, smiling, after seeing my expression.

I nod as if I knew all along what was happening.

The gilded door opens and I recognize that it is a lift. He gestures for me to step inside. He taps a few commands onto his PAD and then puts it away in his pocket. The gilded door closes and we begin to descend.

"It's beautiful," I say, looking at the ornate scrollwork and mirroring around us.

"A replica of an ancient ancestor's house back on Earth," Aldous says.

When the lift stops, Aldous gestures toward the door. "Your rooms. His highness wishes for you to take some time to relax and refresh yourself before dinner this evening. Your luggage has already arrived."

"When is dinner?" I ask.

"Forty minutes. I will return to collect you at that time," he says.

"Thank you, Aldous. That will be all for now," I say, doing my best imitation of the wife of the president of a mining company I once knew and thought of as the most elegant person I'd ever met. I had the feeling I'd be using that particular imitation a lot for a while.

The gilded lift door opens on a small hallway.

I step out and the lift closes behind me.

There is a door immediately to my left and one further down the hall. The walls are the same gold and silver pattern as the other hallways only, here, I can tell, the gold and silver are real. Just to my left, in the middle of the hallway is a waist high table with a circular mirror above it.

Both the doors slide open when I take another step. From the door on the right, a pale blue light plays on the floor. I walk to that one and I can see that it leads to a descending spiral staircase. At the bottom of the staircase, I can see a huge tub sunken into the floor. It faces an enormous window that looks out onto what seems to be the ocean beyond. When I get to the bottom of the staircase, I can see that the walls are filled with shelves and recessed cupboards with soaps and scents and moisturizers and creams as well as towels and the kinds of loose-fitting clothing that I've seen rich people prefer for sleeping.

The room holds only the tub, which could easily fit three of me. My biggest apartment could fit into the space.

Now that I'm close to it, I can see that the window isn't looking out into the ocean of the planet, but instead an aquarium. Here, he has collected tropical fish from Earth. More than one of each, in fact. As I step close I can make out sharks and manta rays and fish with such exotic stripes they seem more painted than alive.

Now that I'm on floor level, I can see that there is a partition made of dark wood along the other wall. I slide it open to discover two things—one, that it doesn't just appear to be wood, which I would expect considering that trees with this much dark wood are mostly a thing of the past on just about all worlds, hence the fad with rich people to make everything out of fake wood which always felt like the plastic that it was, and two, that the partition leads to the other room.

This is where the door that was to my left leads. A spiral staircase just like the other descends from above to the floor where I'm standing. In this room there are the same shelves and recessed cupboards as in the other room, only here they contain books. Books made of actual paper. I pull one out thinking that it will be a blank, meant to show the vast wealth of the man who owns this place—that he can have what are easily thousands of what appear to be actual paper and wood bound books just in his guest room alone, but no. The book I pull down has words printed on the pages. It is a real book, this one apparently a novel by someone named Verne. I pull down three more from random spots and they are all different. They are real books. A vast fortune, enough to buy two or three planets worth, sitting on these shelves.

Where the sunken tub was in the other room, this one contains a huge bed with a massive wooden headboard and huge pillars at the four corners. Just like the tub, it is arranged to look at a giant bubble window that looks out into the tank. I recognize a manta ray that I had spotted earlier because of a gash on one of its huge wings pass by. The thick comforter on the bed is a dark blue background with silver and gold stars woven into it. There are twice as many pillows here as I have ever seen in my life to this point.

Along the other wall are three dark wooden cabinets. I open them to find hundreds of shirts that I can tell are exactly my size arranged by hue, and just as many pants that I will bet are exquisitely tailored to my precise measurements. Three tuxedos, and enough coats and jackets to supply a small army finish out the wardrobe. There are shoes that go all the way from informal slippers through heavy skiing boots, and all without any labels so I'm guessing they are handmade just for me.

I go to the bed and sit down and discover that it is as soft and giving as I had hoped it would be. It's hard not to think of the way you remember your childhood bed being perfect no matter how it was in reality. As soon as the sensor feels pressure on the bed, the lights in both rooms dim and the massive area is washed in the blue light of the colossal tank beyond the bubble windows. A display just next to the window lets me know the current time and the temperature of the room in the same silverish-blue of the water so that the information blends into the room without being jarring.

I find myself just sitting, staring at all of it, thinking about how I have been in the offices and bedrooms of some of the most powerful people who have ever existed, and I have never seen anything even close to this level.

The bath is keyed to my body temperature reading it from my bare feet on the tiles. From that, they determine the perfect water temperature with which to fill the bath. I imagine many people might feel strange about getting naked in front of a giant fish tank, but it is the single most lovely place I've ever been naked before in my life, and the number of places where I've been naked is staggering to consider.

I slide in and soak for thirty minutes, then dress in one of the tuxedos. I'm just finishing the bow tie when a tiny soothing chime sounds.

The display on the wall lets me know that Aldous is in the elevator asking for permission to enter. It tells me that I have to say "yes" out loud to allow him to. I consider for a second saying "no" simply to go along with the headiness of the power of the moment, but then I say "Yes."

I walk up the stairs to meet him. He cocks his head to the side and makes a final adjustment to my bow tie. I feel both comforted and a little put off in the moment because I can tell that his gesture is not for me, but to make sure everything is nice for his employer.

He gestures for me to follow him through the door and back onto the gilded lift.

# THE PAST

"All I'm saying is, this is more money than you've ever gotten before, my darling," Thomas says, then blows out a huge cloud of smoke. He only does it for the retro look. Got a guy out in the burbs who makes them special for him from some plant that he grows. Supposed to keep him calm.

"That's outer rim, though."

"Well, yeah, it is," Thomas says, inhaling again, then blowing another cloud of smoke. "Sure, yeah, it is, but the thing is this—this is a lot of money. And he's paying the transport. First class, my love. First. Class."

"It's a fucking freezer, Thomas—it sort of doesn't matter if it's gold plated or not."

"The drugs are different," he says. "They say you don't have the jitters afterwards with this first class stuff, honey."

Out the window is Los Angeles. Or, at least, it would be, if it wasn't obscured by a thick soup of soot.

"Look, forget it. That's a different business altogether. Just get me another film."

"Well, see, that's part of the problem, my darling. You know that last month Marshall came out with the new A-380s, yeah?" Thomas says, stubbing his cigarette out.

"So?"

"Don't be naïve, love. You know what I mean," Thomas says. "The

380s work. I know a guy who knew a guy who was one of the testers. Says the ass on them is beyond realistic. Julius down at Saller Brothers says by next year you can get them in any color you want. Maybe even child models."

"Disgusting," I say.

"Turn your nose up at it all you want, you know what it means. Pardon me for saying it, dear, but who wants to pay top dollar for a Feelie with a real person, no matter how beyond gorgeous and plucked within an inch of his life that model may be, when they can spend just a little bit more and take home a pleasure machine that will suck them off 24/7 without ever complaining?"

"What I do is—,"

"Yes, my darling, the art of the fantasy. Don't forget that I was the one who found you in obscurity giving hand jobs to beat cops to stop them from hauling you in as a vagrant because you couldn't produce papers. It's been you and me from jump. However, my sweetness, the writing, so to speak, is on the wall. I think it is time to sell the stock while there is still interest, if you know what I mean, my darling."

I shake my head but don't look at him.

Somewhere down the hall, the moaning starts. Another audition. Some kid hoping his particular combination of ass, cock, mouth and feet will get him off the streets. Probably used to sneak into Feelies thinking, "I can do that." Might even have seen one or two of mine.

# OLVER

"Mister Van Ryan?" Aldous says, gesturing for me to step out of the lift once it has stopped. I nod at him and step out. He gestures to his left and I see two huge doors painted white and covered in golden scrollwork. The lift doors close and I'm left standing in the hallway alone.

Almost instantly, though, the doors swing open and I smell food. I walk through the doors into a large dining room. The table is big enough for eight, and there is a large floral arrangement in the center. The walls are covered in murals showing men on horseback riding boldly across deserts and beaches. The far wall has another set of double doors. Just to my left is a smaller single door made to blend in with the wall. It swings opens and a woman comes out holding a tray. On it is two delicate crystal stemmed glasses. Each is filled with a golden liquid.

I take one and she bows slightly. She walks toward the far end of the room and stands near that head of the table. The double doors swing open. In walks a man slightly taller than me with brown skin and jet black hair swept back from his forehead. His white uniform is impressive without being showy. I suddenly feel underdressed.

"Mister James Van Ryan, may I present his royal highness, General Karzen Olver," the woman says. I don't know if I'm supposed to bow or what, so I bend a bit at the waist. "General Olver, your guest, Mister James Van Ryan." He shocks me by returning the exact same bow. Then he walks toward me and extends his hand. "I'm so very pleased to see you arrived safely," he says. His accent is what they would have called British, back before that country became the 53rd state of the American empire.

"Thank you," is all I can think to say. He takes my hand and kisses it lightly, squeezes gently, then releases. He turns on his heel and gestures back toward the table. "Please, sit." He then walks to a chair just to the side of the head of one end and pulls it back. I sit and he moves the chair back into place. He then sits at the head of the table. Immediately we are brought a carafe of dark red wine and fat goblets. He pours generously for me, then himself. He looks at the wine under the light, then brings it just under his nose. Then he takes a sip. He closes his eyes and nods to the woman who then leaves the room. "Please," he says, gesturing toward my goblet.

I've had lots of wines, lots of gins, lots of vodkas...I am no stranger to all the various ways that people make their alcohol. This was a different taste than I'd ever had, though. I couldn't help staring at the wine with my eyebrows furled a bit.

"We grow the grapes here. However, being so far down in the water, and surrounded on all sides by yeast spores, they take on their own particular flavor. Our yields are small, but the wine is sought after for its unique flavor. What do you think?" Olver asks.

"It's good," I say. He smiles and we both take another sip.

"How was your journey?" he asks. The door to the side opens up and a man comes in bearing a basket of bread and two small bottles. It turned out to be a flatbread of some kind and sets up a bowl with oil and then dark, dark vinegar swimming in it.

"Long, but not too bad," I say

"And did you have a chance to bathe and rest? Aldous took care of your luggage?"

The bread is soft and wonderful, the oil is fruity, and the vinegar has a just-shy of overpowering bite. It all goes perfectly with the wine. I'm sure that is no accident.

"It is really something to take a bath while fish look in on you," I say.

Olver laughs. "I can imagine it will take some getting used to. Tell me, during your flight out—you were in cryosleep, yes?"

I nod and take another sip of my wine. I find the more I have of it, the more I want the taste on my tongue, like the first time I ever had wine made of muscadines.

"Did you dream?" he asks.

"They say you aren't supposed to," I answer.

"That isn't an answer," he says with a smile.

"I…I think I did. But I'm not sure." I'm lying.

"You lie. But that's okay," he says, his smile growing. He leans back from the table. "You may protect your mysteries as long as you like. They are yours, of course." The words sound jagged but his manner is still loose.

"Have you?" I ask.

"Pardon?" he asks.

"Gone in cryosleep?"

"No," he says. "I'm sure the idea of me leaving the planet would send Aldous into fits of rage. So far, no business has taken me away from my home," as he says this, he gestures all around us. "This is why I was curious. Some of my guests over the years have reported dreaming, but all of the literature on the subject suggests perhaps they are assigning those dreams after the fact."

The door opens again and in comes another young man with two large bowls. Behind him the woman from before comes in carrying another carafe of wine. I had hardly noticed, but we'd already polished off

24

the first.

"How long has he worked for you?" I ask. The bowls are set before us. In them is a dark soup.

"Who, Aldous?" he asks. He cocks his head to the side as he calculates. "This will be his tenth year, if I am remembering correctly. His predecessor had been one of my father's counselors who managed to escape the destruction." Olver takes a spoonful of the soup, and I follow suit. The broth is rich and peppery. "There is an old expression that I quite like for its colorfulness. When someone is as close to someone else as Aldous is to me, they used to say, 'he knows where all the bodies are buried.'" He laughs. I smile in return. "If there is anyone who knows where absolutely all of my bodies are buried, it is Aldous."

We both have our soup in silence for a while. Olver catches me looking at the murals. "Supposedly," he says, "these depict ancient members of my own house. Relatives from before the time when man set foot away from Earth for the first time. Do you enjoy history?"

"I like it when people tell it to me," I say. "I don't much like reading it." Again, the soup goes perfectly with the wine, and again, I'm sure it is no accident. I look down to find my bowl nearly empty and most of the wine gone. I tell myself I should slow down. Even with my tolerance, I'm already starting to feel dizzy.

"Where are you in all of that?" I ask, gesturing vaguely toward the murals.

He chews for a moment, then cocks his head to the side. "I suppose they must be at least starting to make the one that depicts my tenure as the leader here. My part of the family's story. I haven't seen it."

"What do you think it will show?" I ask.

He's quiet again. "In my youth," Olver says, "I was trained as a mech pilot. That was my service to the colony. I imagine that will form a great

25

deal of it."

"I've never met anyone before who did that," I say. I've been with men who were in the armed forces before, and played many characters who were in the forces themselves, but somehow mech pilot had never been among those. "That must be a powerful feeling...having tons of armor around you like that. Trading in your small body for a much larger, more powerful one," I say, then sip my wine.

"Would you like to see?" Olver asks. "After dinner, perhaps we will go down to the hangar."

I try not to show that the possibility excites me.

"And what else will you show me after dinner?" I ask. I didn't mean it to be innuendo, but I hear it the moment I say it.

Olver smiles. I like his smile. "Perhaps," he says, "I will show you the monster I keep below." From any other man, I'd suspect this of being crude banter, but somehow I suspect that for this man, it is not.

The moment dinner is finished, Olver stands. Immediately Aldous comes to his side. They whisper for a moment and then Aldous leaves. Olver had been holding his napkin in his hand but as soon as we are alone, he places it on the table. He looks at me a moment, then walks down the table to me.

"Let's go for a walk," he says.

"Here," Olver says as we exit the pod out onto a huge grand street. He's handing me a coat. As I slip my shoulders into it, I notice it doesn't feel like anything I've ever felt before. Seeing my face, Olver settles the coat on my shoulders and says, "We call them whales for lack of a better term. Very large sea life...not quite mammals. This is made from their topmost layer of skin and the fur that grows on it. We find that it still

26

retains some of the ability to regulate itself. Opening what you might think of as pours when it's very warm, closing them when it's cold."

I'm not sure whether to be flattered that he would give such a thing to me, or disgusted.

We go a few blocks in silence. I've been places like this before. Shops line the streets, the kinds of shops that you can't even enter without a name journalists would recognize. That's when I notice, though—it's completely empty.

"Where is everyone?" I ask.

"We have the street entirely to ourselves," Olver says. I hear the pride in his voice. This is a show of power intended for me.

"I see," I say. I try to keep the fact that it's working out of my voice.

We walk over a bridge that crests over another street below. From here I can see for what seems like miles, and yet I still can't see the edges of the dome. The sky stretches away from us. I know the air is recycled, but somehow, seeing the blue sky above and the horizon dotted with trees, the pathways of rose bushes below, it all works on me. After the maze of mega skyscrapers that was Los Angeles when I left it, this feels like something out of a storybook. Something you'd read to a kid.

He puts his hand on the small of my back and my shoulders relax immediately. All I can think is, how did he know? Then I remember that I've done more than a few interviews where they ask about those kinds of things. He's probably read them. Still, even that level of effort is sort of sweet.

"How far down are we, exactly?" I ask.

"Does it matter?" he asks, leaning on the railing with me. "You are here. That is what is important." I turn to see his face and he leans in and kisses me. Just a quick peck, really; nothing heavy. It's nice. "You close your eyes when you kiss," he says.

"Only when I'm being kissed. When I'm the one doing the—," I start.

"Yes, I know," he says, kissing me again a bit harder.

Around the corner, for a split second as we cross from one street to the next, I see a child race from a doorway to another. I turn to remark on it, but the second I do, Olver steps in front of me. "Over here is the street where most of our weavers reside," he says and points back the direction we were going.

I follow him and we look at several displays of blankets and the embroidered jackets I've seen people wear in videos from ancient homeworld.

"Where are the weavers?" I ask. "I would like to buy one of these jackets."

He takes the one I've been touching off the rack and holds it out for me to slide into. I slide out of the whale coat and into the cloth one.

"But I should pay…"

"Nonsense," Olver says. "I will handle the payments. You needn't worry about anything."

As he's talking, over his shoulder, I see what I assume are his forces are sweeping back along the street where I saw the child earlier. He sees the direction I'm looking and without looking that way himself, he says, "you are very important to me. Your safety is very important to me. They are just making sure that no one is here to harm you."

I smile. He smiles back at me and kisses me. The jacket fits beautifully, and I feel warm. I can't help but wonder, though, what he means by harm—who would want to harm me? Why? He kisses me again and puts his hand on the small of my back and we're off down another side street, the guards following at a respectful distance.

28

Later, we're standing next to the tank, when, out of the murk, something huge drifts by. I take a step back without thinking and directly into his arms.

"Do not be alarmed," he says. "This is one of my most prized possessions." He lets go of me and steps closer to the tank and caresses the glass. "Kleister 765 has three worlds in its habitable zone. There is only one, though, that has a large enough supply of water to truly be what we might call an ocean." I dimly remember what he's talking about from some class I took once. "It was the first place, you'll remember, to confirm the idea that—," as he says this, the bulk drifts slowly up to the glass and I can make out a large body and long, thin shadows extending down below it. Whatever it is, it is easily fifty feet long, maybe more. "— what we used to call squid on Earth were the most common form of life on planets that had bodies of water. Now, of course, that is so commonly accepted that even the uneducated know it. Then, though, it was the great great grandmother of this very animal who unlocked that small corner of the puzzle." It comes very close to the glass and I can see its purple and pearlescent-white skin ripple with the light from the room. I know it isn't, but for a second it seems to be reacting to his caress through the glass. His eyes have gone misty as he stares at the enormous squid. "Of all the things I have in my collection," he says, "it is the most beautiful. The most meaningful."

He doesn't look at me, but I can tell he is.

"Everyone collects something, a wise man once told me," Olver continues. "I never really understood it until very recently." He gestures toward a panel and the lighting goes even dimmer. Soon, the only light left in the whole room comes from the animal's skin. Though the room's temperature is perfectly controlled, I feel a chill. Olver puts his arm around my shoulder. "Power, this same man said, is the ability to collect the things you want, no matter how outrageous. Women, land…men. Power is the ability to have what you want delivered to you without having to take it by force." The animal makes a pass very close to the window then, with a huge jolt, jets away into the darkness. The room around us goes all but black. "I thought long and hard about this and I decided that I wanted to be a collector of life. To make sure that what I gathered to me were things that were necessary for life."

"And how does that fit in," I say, gesturing toward the window.

"Well, to quote another very smart man, biodiversity is a reward all its own. However, it is also a reminder."

"Of?" I ask.

"That something with sheer raw power can be a thing of beauty."

Later, further down into the station's core, a huge door opens onto an enormous hangar. Immediately the chill air attacks. I pull the whale jacket closer around me. He gestures for me to walk ahead of him. The lights come up and I'm staring at what looks like a fifteen-foot tall person decked out in thick armor plating. I step back and he laughs, putting his hand on my lower back. We walk closer to it. No part of it moves, but I could swear that it is watching us.

It is predominantly the gray of carbon fiber, but here and there are accents of purple and black, the colors mostly favored by the colonies during the uprisings. All along the skin of the giant metal warrior are slashes and pock marks where it has taken damage. The head resembles an ancient Samurai demon mask I saw in a documentary once.

The overall effect is that I am standing before some angry God which will decide to obliterate me at any moment.

"What is it?" I ask.

"This? This is my mobile armor. Or, at least, it was," he said. He waits a moment, then says, "Back when they would let me…" whatever he was thinking drifts off with a sigh. "I believe people back on Earth used to call them 'mecha' in the last war," he says, turning away from it.

"You piloted it?"

"Yes," he says. He looks up at it, and places his hand reverently on the machine's "foot."

"What's that like?" I ask.

"I'm not sure I understand," he says, that devastating smile flashing across his face.

"Well, I mean, it looks like a person, so when you're piloting it, it's kind of like…"

"Ah," he says, "yes. Was I aware, you're asking, of the feeling of this giant lump of alloys and carbon fibers being a second, huge body? In a way, I suppose. After all, if it experienced damage, that damage made me aware of it, much like pain makes someone aware of their own body." I don't think he's aware of it, but he's stroking the machine's "foot" as he talks. "And a good pilot does tend to become one with the machine. It has been so long, though, since all of that unpleasantness."

"Why do you keep it?" I ask.

"Sentimentality," he says.

I follow him out of the hangar, resisting the urge to look behind us as we walk away. I don't want to know if the machine is staring at us as we leave.

The lift arrives and he gestures for me to step inside.

"So," Olver says, "what do you think of my little station?" His grin is infectious, but I decide not to give away too much too soon.

"I like it," I say. I can tell he wanted a much bigger reaction. He nods, presses a button, and the lift doors close. We begin to move downward.

"Of course, this isn't all. Soon I will take you down to our production facilities."

I nod.

He shakes his head and laughs.

"What are you laughing at?" I ask.

"You."

"What about me is funny?" I ask.

"You're cautious with me, you hold back…almost as if you expect I might attack you at some point."

"I wasn't aware that's how—"

"Come now," he said, taking my hand. "There's no reason to lie. I suspect that this is the way you deal with everyone. Always at the ends of your fingertips; no one gets any closer than that."

"We've only just met," I say. The lift comes to a stop. When the door opens, we're back in the small hallways just outside the rooms he's given me. He gestures for me to step out. When I do, he follows. The doors close behind him.

"Is that true?" he asks. "Or have we known each other through lifetime after lifetime?" He steps past me, his shoulder brushing against mine. He walks through the doorway that leads down the steps to the enormous bathtub.

"You're a romantic," I say without following.

"Am I?" he says.

I'm standing there for a moment and then I follow. Once I get to the top of the stairs he is already at the bottom. I come down the stairs slowly.

"You should rest. Tomorrow I will take you even further. I will show you wonders," he says. Before I've made it to the bottom of the stairs he has turned and walks through to the other room. When I get to the arch that divides the two, he is already ascending the other stairs. "Goodnight," he says over his shoulder.

"Goodnight," I say but the door is already closing behind him.

I've been lying on the bed for an hour trying to calm down. I'm exhausted, but the day has been too huge. The electricity of it surges through me.

I draw a bath and slide into the enormous tub. I'm thinking about taking matters into my own hands just to find some release and then sleep.

I can finally admit that I was afraid I wouldn't be attracted to him. I had convinced myself that I would somehow get through it. I had before. When you work in the industry, you find yourself partnered with people you have to pretend to be attracted to all the time. I had decided I would do my best to get through it.

But I don't have to.

He's magnetic. His dark eyes, his perfectly groomed beard, his dark skin. But it goes deeper than just his features; the way he carries his power, his subtle strength, his assuredness.

I want him.

It is at that exact moment that the chime sounds and I see that he is at the door.

The door slides open without me touching the controls.

"May I?" Olver asks, stepping in. His robe is loosely tied at his waist, the thick white cotton of it draped around his tight body.

I wonder if I'm supposed to stand, even though I'm in the tub, or not. What is the proper thing to do?

"Yes," I say. Some part of me wants to say something clever like, "it's your palace" like one of my characters would in a movie, but something

33

about this feels drastically different than all of those times.

It's been a very long time since I was shy about my body, or nervous about sex. Somehow, in this moment, I'm both.

Olver comes down the stairs like a lion. His movements powerful, assured, inevitable. He moves over to the bath and kneels down beside it. He puts his hand in the water and rests it on my knee all without breaking eye contact.

"Don't let your people see you just sitting on the floor like that," I say.

"If they have any opinions on the subject, it would be wise for them to keep such thoughts to themselves," Olver says. "Besides," he continues as he stirs the water a bit with his hand, "I have cleared everyone on this floor away for the evening."

"We're alone?" I ask.

He nods. "We are alone."

I take his hand and pull him toward me. I kiss him deeply the way I've wanted to for hours. I stand and pull him up with me. I untie his sash and then slip his robe from around him letting it drop to the floor. His body is exactly as I pictured it. I pull him into the tub with me.

"What was it like, the first time?" I ask. The sheets are cool and soft against my legs.

"The first time...?" he asks in return. I nuzzle my chin into his smooth chest and pull my body closer to his. All the while, some part of me is thinking that this is crazy, being this open with someone, especially after all I've done.

"In the armor, the first time you piloted it, what was it like?" I ask.

"Ah," he says and laughs a bit. I find I like the way it rumbles through his chest. "Well, that's a long story. Are you sure you want it?"

he asks. I nod against him and he puts both arms around me. "It was an accident, you see. I had no intention of ever joining the military at all. My older brother, he was the one who wanted fame and glory for the family name. All I ever wanted was to be left alone in our grand library." He rubs my upper arm. "Three weeks into the rebellion, the Earth forces smashed that library destroying every book my family had ever held dear." I think for a moment about what he might have been like had he gotten his wish; a scholarly man, the second son of an outer rim nobleman entitled to nothing but his books. "You see, back then, there were land masses, here. Few, true enough, but they did exist. The Earth forces decided just a few weeks into the rebellion that the idea of proportional response was not something they were interested in. I suppose our poor luck was that, at least from their point of view, we were the next in a long, long line of rebellious colonies, and they were stretched thin. As you well know, when people are desperate, they often make bad choices." I put my hand on his chest.

"So it was in one of those spectacularly overpowered raids that the last land mass, the one that was our home for two hundred years was reduced to rubble. I wish I could say that I was glorious that day, but I had actually faked being sick to stay home from school. When the first raid sirens called, letting us know that Earth forces ships had begun their deceleration, I was in my bed, doing what young men that age tend to do when they can find a moment alone." He laughs a bit and so do I. "I was very close to completing my little act of rebellion, as a matter of fact, when those sirens began. This is why I paid perhaps less attention to them than they deserved. 'This is merely a drill,' I told myself and continued on with what I was doing. Even as those cruisers were coming to end our way of life, I was feverishly dreaming of Ossad, the son of one of our house cleaners. He was a year or two older than

me, I think, and I used to hide and watch him at his mopping or dust-
ing. When he thought he was alone in a room, he would sing to himself
and sometimes even dance, his beautiful bare feet making precise little
movements. I suppose it is lucky that I was under the sheets that day,
something of a luxury for what I was doing—one is never alone in a
house with servants, you know, especially when one is in bed." I can feel
him shake as he remembers. Again, some part of me keeps saying to
pull away, to stop listening, but his voice has me mesmerized.

"Should I be jealous?" I ask.

He sighs. "No. Ossad died that day as there was no room for the
servants in the family transport. All of them were vaporized in the attack."

"I'm sorry," I say.

"No need to be. It wasn't your doing. Some young man, his heart
full of the bile that he was told about us in the colonies and our desire
for independence, was at the controls of that drone. It is him that should
be ashamed. Many days I have thought about using the resources under
my command and finding out his name. The names of those who were
piloting those remote ships that day. Of reaching out and ending their
lives wherever they may be." The icy edge that crept into his voice made
me shiver. "But that is not our way, and they are long dead, most likely,"
he says, rubbing my upper arm again. "One of the maids came storm-
ing into the room. Just as it was lucky I was under the sheets that day,
it is also lucky she came in when she did and not a moment later. At
that point, I would have been…shall we say…unable to stop what I was
doing." He moves one of his feet up under mine, a purely unconscious
gesture, I am sure, but the simple sweetness of it makes even more of
my defenses fall away. "At any rate, she began throwing clothes into one
of my suitcases and urged me to get up and get dressed. She uttered the

special code word we'd all been taught that meant that this was not a drill, and that the danger was grave. At any other time, I'd have had a bit of a dilemma on my hands—namely, to get up and have her see what I'd been doing, or to try to lie in bed until things had calmed down. Even with the seriousness of the situation, I opted for the second. I told her that this was surely a drill, that I was certain there weren't any Earth forces ships closing in on us from above. Her hysterics only grew. Eventually I was…calmed down…enough to move. By then she had packed as much as she could into the suitcase and was dragging me, in my underwear, down the hallway by my arm. The family transport was down in the docking garage and when I got down there, my mother and two younger sisters were all in the back seat. The bodyguards gestured frantically for me to hurry. That's when it hit me that things were serious. Our two closest bodyguards, Sylas, who was only a few years older than me, and Zekiah, who was like a kind uncle, were stone faced in every situation. I'd once seen them take down a man trying to kill my father with a single gesture, neither of them even having to readjust their sunglasses, after. Yet here they were practically screaming for me to get in the transport. Once I was in, they slammed the doors closed and the transport screamed from the sudden acceleration. I never saw our palace or any of those people who had worked so hard to make it a home again." His pause went on for a while. "My father had given orders to come directly to the military command center. From there he was going to get us off the planet with his command cruiser. This was, I have come to learn, something no commander is allowed to do. Families, no matter the danger of the situation, are supposed to take the family cruiser. He didn't care—he wanted us safe behind that thick armored hull with him at the guns, a squadron of pilots in the mobile armor lead by my oldest brother defending us. We arrived and after a brief exchange with him, we were all shuffled down to the command ship. My mother shoved me into one of the pilot suits to cover my nakedness as the girls were being strapped in. I was, to be honest, numb with fear. I wish I could say I had the desire to fight, to defend our way of life, but all I felt was the desire to hide, to wish all this wasn't happening. I remember, though, that as we were shoved on board the transport, there was one mobile armor in the belly of the ship. I asked my father about it, but he brushed my question aside. Soon, we were all strapped in and he gave the command for the ship to take off."

He pats my arm and sits up. I sit up with him. "As we rose to orbit, I saw the cruisers. Massive things, unbelievably big to my young eyes. I saw my brother and his squadron of men fight valiantly, but one by one, they were destroyed. I happened to be sitting closer to the flight deck than my mother or sisters, so I heard when my father said that the last armor, my brother, the hope of our family, had been destroyed. The transport was without any escort and the pilots still needed time to get the ship ready to accelerate. The thought sunk in—we weren't going to make it. Then I remembered the mobile armor that we had in the belly of the ship. Because I was my father's son, I had been given very basic training in how to pilot one. I must admit, I was never very good at it, but I could at least fly one. In my panic, in my numbness, I didn't realize what I was doing until I was already back down in the launch bay staring at the giant thing. I climbed aboard, started it up, and was just about to break free from the travel restraints when my father came into the bay. You see, once you get past a certain point in the warm up, a signal goes to whatever launch control board there is that you have started the thing up. He came running once he noticed. I knew that if I heard his voice, I would break, lose my nerve, and that would be that. So, before he could say anything, and, indeed, before the warmup was complete, I pulled the lever that released the mobile armor into space. I'll never know what his last words were to me because no sooner had I launched from the bay than the transport carrying my whole family was destroyed. Had I waited even just one more second, I would have been, too. As it was, the armor took a great deal of damage, but the explosion knocked me so far away from the wreckage that the Earth forces never found me. They thought the armor was just floating jetsam from the transport. I imagined that I would charge into the armor, that I would launch at the Earth ships and make them pay for destroying my beautiful brother. Instead, I powered down and floated in orbit until the Earth drones left. I watched them bombard my planet for hours feeling helpless." I put my arms around him and he holds me back.

"I'm so sorry. You did the right thing, though," I say.

"Did I?"

"You were a boy piloting one mobile suit—what could you have done against a squad of planet killers?"

"I suppose," he whispered. After a long time, he leans back and sighs. "Eventually the all-clear was sounded, after the drones sped away. I knew enough to know how to follow a beacon, so I followed the message down to the surface and the safety of the remaining rebels. They were a faction that had not had my father's faith in the basic humanity of the Earth forces, so they had hidden deep under the ocean. I joined them immediately, and they were happy for the legitimacy that I brought them—the young prince has survived and sides with us, they could say. This rallied many who were on the fence to their cause. The story of the slaughter of my family was also a powerful rallying cry. They trained me to pilot the armor, painted it in my family's colors as a battlefield reminder, and here we are." He gets out of bed and walks to the window, his naked body powerful and even more beautiful in motion than it had been lying down. "I'm sorry, I've probably bored you back to sleep."

"No," I say. I lean back against the headboard and watch his back as he stares out into the depths of the enormous tank until I fall back into sleep.

He shifts a bit in the bed, and I wake up.

"You're awake," he says.

"How can you tell?"

"Your breathing changed."

"Why are you awake?" I ask.

His arm goes around my shoulders and he pulls me to him. His body is lean and his warmth is more of a glow than a furnace, as some men can be.

"Sometimes it is difficult to sleep," he says. At the very edge of his voice is pain. I pull myself even closer to him.

"Now that I'm here," I start, "may I ask why you chose me?"

"You're very direct," he says.

"Is that a problem?" I ask.

"No," he says. "I'm just not used to it anymore. Everyone defers to me."

"Is that not something you like?" I ask.

"When I was younger, it thrilled me. The older I get, though, the more I long for someone to tell me the truth. To tell me what they honestly feel."

The room grows so quiet I can hear the water moving through the pipes in the walls. For a moment, I think he may have fallen asleep.

"I chose you because I think you are one of the most beautiful men I have ever seen."

"You watched my movies," I say. Logically, I know he has—otherwise he wouldn't know of me. Still, on some level, I thought perhaps one of his staff had maybe…I'm not sure. Though I know that all males masturbate regardless of age, somehow it hadn't crossed my mind that maybe he did.

"As I said, my family was gone and I had to assume power from an early age. Once one is in power, courting becomes…difficult. This is compounded when one's culture is not exactly accepting of the sexuality I was rapidly coming to understand was my own."

"Did you date women?" I ask.

"Yes," he sighs. "and, so that you know, there have been a few men along the way. It couldn't last with any of them, of course, but there were."

"Why didn't it last?" I ask.

"There would be the assumption of power that would come along with the relationship. A servant wouldn't have to be particularly sharp-eyed to notice that a particular mech pilot lieutenant was spending quite a bit of time in the royal apartments. They might then communicate that to someone who might communicate that to someone and so on and so on until people began to treat that particular pilot as if they were a head of state, their merest whim a command. Surely, you can see the problem."

"I can," I say. "And so someone had to be brought in from outside to…solve the problem." I let my hand slide across his tight belly and down lower. He laughs.

"That was the thinking among my most trusted advisors, yes. Someone from outside who would not assume any power came with the relationship. And so the search began."

"How romantic," I say, hoping he can hear the smile in my voice.

"Indeed," he says, kissing the top of my head.

"And why me in particular?" I ask.

"Because you are the best. They never asked me, and I'm not sure I would have told them, but you were always a favorite. When your name was on the list, I had to hide my excitement. I picked you immediately."

"No one else?"

"Initially, the group that decided to take on this particular…problem…had wanted to invite a group of others and audition them in various ways before presenting me with a short list," he says.

"Oh?"

"Fortunately, sanity prevailed and they figured out without my intervention how I would have detested that solution. It is, however, exactly the way they tend to think about most things."

"It has been a long time since I was asked to audition for anything," I say. "I wonder how I would have done through their tests," I say.

He laughs, "Do you know the correct fork to use during the salad course?"

I laugh, too.

"And so what now? Am I to be kept in the apartments as a secret?" This comes out colder than I intend.

"No," he says. "No, we are done with that."

"I'm glad to hear it," I say, pulling against him even tighter. I can hear his breath fill his lungs. "Why the sudden change? I'm sure there were others who were far more worthy of it."

"No," he says. "There weren't."

"That's very nice of you to say, but we have only known each other a short while."

"I can already tell. You have pain. It…resonates…with my own. I can already feel that." His voice changes, grows a sudden hard edge to it.

"How can you tell?" I ask.

"I knew it the instant I saw you," he says, the hard edge growing cold. "I...hate...the Earth and everything it stands for...so much..." His voice grows more restrained with each syllable, until it can barely escape at the last. "It may not be the same for you, but I can tell there is something in your life that you have just as much anger about...that you feel just as much alienation from..." I don't know how I know, but I can tell he is on the verge of crying. I wonder at so much emotion coming so quickly, but I'm also swept up in it.

I shush him as I lean up to kiss him.

He's right. Something in me vibrates at the same level I feel in him. Like beehives located near one another, their angry, panicky, swarming buzz sounding at the same note. I move to straddle him while still kissing him. Then he is inside me, and together we ride his anger and pain like a wave until eventually it dies down to a low, warm buzzing, and then, finally, both exhausted, we make it to sleep.

# LIKE SOMETHING

# FROM A DREAM

Day 12 of what the man who has told me to call him "coach" calls my "new life."

How he keeps a straight face when he says that, I will never know.

Today I learned about how I can run.

I learned I can run a mile in 8 minutes.

"Coach" says that's not bad. He says I'll get better.

It felt good to run.

To open up.

To be nothing but a set of legs moving.

To not be the boy who gets hit.

To not be the boy who gets screamed at.

"Coach" says that there are only two kind of people in the world.

The raw and the cooked.

He says you get busy living or you get busy dying.

He says there is a world where we're all beautiful and nobody ever has to do anything wrong.

But this world, he says, isn't that one.

Which one are you? "Coach" asks.

If it's eat or be eaten, then you want to be the guy with the gun," "Coach" says.

That's what we're building.

A life support unit for a gun that points where it's aimed.

A mobile weapons platform with a dick.

I wonder if he's ever thought about opening up a greeting card company.

Some of these little nuggets should be on bumper stickers.

I make sure not to smirk at that thought, though.

I made the mistake of smirking just once at one of his jokes.

The beatings my old man doled out were intense. I used to think world class.

I knew nothing of how cruel and precise the horror someone could deliver unto me could be.

So now I make no expressions.

Dad, can you put the cat out?—I didn't know it was on fire "Coach" says and guffaws.

I say nothing.

Why couldn't the bicycle stand up by itself?—It was two tired "Coach" yells and roars.

Stone faced.

Don't trust atoms—They make up everything!

Nothing. Nada. Zip.

I am nothing more than legs moving.

The whole universe is nothing but legs moving.

Today I learned that I can run.

One mile in 8 minutes.

"Coach" says that's not terrible. For a Nazi cocktail waitress, he says, it's a little above average. For a part-time terrorist candy striper at a morgue it is damn near outstanding, he says.

Tomorrow I will run faster.

# THE PAST

The night before my first trip outside the solar system.

"They say you're not supposed to dream on the stuff, but I have," the guy says to me leaning his forehead against my left hip. I guess I'm supposed to want him to keep going until I get off, but at this point I could take it or leave it, honestly. I've ridden that ride so many times I can imagine myself there if I wanted to. He doesn't even have to be in the room.

"When the stuff hits you, you go out instantly. As close to brain dead as a person can get without tipping over, they tell us."

But, because I've been thinking about it, I asked him about hyper-sleep. That had lead to us talking about what he kept calling "the juice" or "the stuff." The cocktail of chemicals sent through your veins to bring you as close to death as possible before the temperature in the pod went below zero.

He's a pilot. Baby face with huge hands, which is one of my favorite types. He's stuck doing the Moon to Earth run when what he really wants to be is outbound from the solar system at half the speed of light, like so many of them.

"There was that one guy in that band. You know the one. Long hair and the leather pants with the cool boots? Anyway, he said he used the stuff to dream and then he woke up and wrote their album. That one that won all the awards." I push his head a bit so his lips go around my

47

cock. He's dumb, but I like the sharp cut of his jawline and the brown of his eyes.

In the morning, I'm due on a short carrier to get me to a station around Jupiter, then outbound to live for a year with a man who likes my work. A "contract" my agent calls it. If it goes well, he says, we'll do more of these. Thinking about how much money the guy is paying for me gets me throbbing. I push the pilot's head down further and I finish up down his throat.

He lays his head against my hip, again.

"Any way, I remember having a dream, this was early on, mind, where I woke up from the freeze but the lid wasn't open. In the dream, I could feel the hoses going down my throat and up inside me from the other end. I could feel the cold in my bones, and my eyes were open. Autodocs played back the spool and said that there was no higher brain function at all during the entire flight, so a dream was impossible. That's what they always tell us," he said, stroking my stomach. "but I know what I felt, and it felt like years that I was trapped in that pod, in constant pain and unable to communicate with anyone for help."

He moves up and spoons in behind me. I pull the covers up over us.

"Delirium, now…that's the scary stuff."

"What's that?" I ask.

He snuggles in to me. "Odds are very low, something like one time in a million, but sometimes someone has a bad reaction to the waking process. The chemicals get a bad mix ratio or the heaters are too close to the skin or something. We don't know, really. Maybe all of the above. But the person, instead of waking up slowly, all docile and a little sick, they come out of the pod raging. Instead of being weak as a kitten, they come out strong as an ox, and in full-on panic. Start lashing out at whatever is close, usually some poor attendant getting paid hourly who

48

was just sitting there monitoring the screens. 'Emergent Delirium' they call it."

"What ends up happening to the person?" I ask.

"In every case I've ever heard of, they have to put them down on the spot."

# SYLAS

The next morning I wake up alone.

He knew enough, though, to put the covers back down after he got out of the bed so that it all stayed warm. I smile at this and snuzzle deeper into the pillow and smile. Maybe, this time...I think.

I get up and walk naked into the other room where I run a bath. Outside the window there is no light, of course, but I imagine that somewhere, above us, there is sun shining on the surface of the water. The bathtub is large enough that I can stretch out fully without touching the sides at all. I sink under the water, close my eyes, and listen to my heartbeat, enjoying the irony of being under water while underwater.

My muscles are starting to unknot and I spend more time in the bath than I normally would. It's only then that I realize that I didn't bother to bring a towel over. I spot the cabinet that I remember them being in. It's not that I have an issue with being seen naked, it's that I'll be treading water all over these beautiful tiles. I know that someone will have to come along and dry all of it up, and that I will have caused that. Still, I can see no other way.

I get out and try to let myself drip as much as possible in one spot. Then I pad over to the wall and open the cupboard. The thick, long towels come in many different colors. I choose a blue one and wrap it around myself. There's almost enough room to wrap twice, in fact.

I walk back to the bed, thinking about what I might do with the day. Will he be alright with me going out to explore? Does he want me to stay here, letting him be the one to introduce me to more of the dome?

On the bed is a beige hooded industrial jumpsuit in my exact size. On top of it is a note that says, "put this on NOW." I look around to see which of the staff might have come in without me seeing. There is no one else in the room. The back of the card says "Trust me." I look back down at the note. It seems so urgent. That's when a click nearby makes me look up.

Along the wall are other cabinets of all sizes.

What I also see is that one of the cabinet doors has slid open to reveal a very dark corridor beyond.

It was a door. A door that is now open.

I'm suddenly very aware that I'm naked and that there is a chance someone is going to come out of this hidden doorway. Part of me is turned on by the idea, the other part of me wants the comfort of some sort of protection. I reach for the jumpsuit and slide it on. As with all such garments, it's designed to go on easily and adapt quickly to lots of different kinds of bodies. It shrinks down to my size fast, moving the excess cloth around to the hood and extra pouches on the thighs. The top button beeps once to let me know it has shrunken itself as far as it can. It's still a bit bulky on me, but also much warmer than I expect it to be.

Out of the darkness inside comes a hand. It snaps loudly at me, then waves me over. I stand still for a moment. I'll be honest—if I was put on a witness stand and asked "why did you go along with any of this?" I couldn't tell you. Something just wouldn't let me not. So I move to the door. Once the jumpsuit feels that I'm moving, it deploys the soles underneath the foot coverings, and the wrists cinch up a bit. I now look like any ordinary average industrial worker in any one of a thousand different fields.

I could be anyone.

Once I'm inside the doorway, the door slides closed behind me.

"Hello?" I say, my voice echoing around me.

In the darkness, someone grabs my arm and pulls me further into the darkness.

It seems like we're walking forever, but because it's so dark, I have lost all bearing of where I might be.

Eventually I can see a slight graying up ahead. As we get closer I can see that it's light.

"Where are we?" I ask.

I'm vehemently shushed and the pulling gets more rough. I can make out the outline of the other person against the light from ahead. The person pulling me is either a very slightly built man or a woman.

My internal clock has gone haywire and I can't tell how long it takes us but eventually the light up ahead is bright enough that I can see clearly the walls and the floor of the tube, and the person in front of me. No wonder they were so hard to make out; their jumpsuit is entirely black with even the zipper blacked out so no light reflects off of it. The only bit of exposed skin is their eyes.

For a second I wonder why they bothered to go to such lengths for stealth when dragging me in my regular bright and reflective clothing behind them. I sense that the person, whoever they are, is in no mood for questions, though.

The hallway ends at a door with a bare bulb above it. The door has no decoration whatsoever and after spending so much time in the mansion, the bare metal seems shocking, hints of danger. The person in front of me removes a glove and places it against the door then waits. I

52

hear the tiniest of scratching sounds, so slight I almost think I may have only dreamed it, but then the person who dragged me here nods. He or she removes a small metal plate next to the doorway revealing a panel of buttons. My escort selects the yellow one and presses, making the door slide aside. I get a whiff of yeast and dirt and see a spiral staircase descending into shadow below.

"Go to the bottom. Sylas will meet you there," the person who brought me here says. I still can't discern male or female from the voice and before I can ask, they disappear into the blackness going back the way we came.

Down the staircase? Or back the other way and forget all of this? I would like to say that I had some manly moment of decision, but the truth is that both ways seemed equally treacherous to me. I choose the stairs more out of curiosity than any kind of conviction. As soon as I'm three steps down, the door slides shut behind me.

Red light comes from below as well as a machine sound that I'd never heard before. The yeast smell increases as I got further down eventually becoming an overpowering memory of being in the kitchen of a bakery. After four twists around, the bottom of the staircase opens out onto a wide, flat floor. Machines, tables, and conveyor belts run in all directions. People in white jumpsuits and smocks with their faces covered by masks move in all directions.

A man with close-cropped black hair, slightly taller than I am, and dressed all in an all-gray jumpsuit much like the one I'm wearing comes up to me. On any other man, his neatly trimmed moustache would seem laughable, but makes me think of him as in charge and powerful.

"Van Ryan," he says in a heavily accented voice.

"Are you Sylas?" I ask.

He nods.

"What is going—?"

"Indulge me and all will be explained. For now, know that you are in no danger and that I will return you to the palace before he knows you are gone," Sylas says. Hard not to hear the note of venom on the word "he."

"What is this place?" I ask. "What is going on here?"

He waves for me to follow him. As we pass by people, I notice they make room for him. Some bow as they stop to let us pass. "This is one of the many yeast factories. They grow it below, in the very bowels of the station, and ship it up to this floor to be processed and then we send it further up to the kitchens to eventually become whatever it is they serve at the tables above."

As a reflex, I nod, even though he's walking in front and can't see me. We reach a door on the far side of the room from the staircase I've just come down and it opens for him. We pass through and when it closes, I heard a sucking sound and my ears pop.

"Though it gives life, so much yeast can also become a nuisance and even harm life if it is not properly controlled," he says. We pass through another door and the same sound comes after. On this side, the room we're in is cold and there are shower stalls to the side. We move through this room into another where there are row upon row of lockers. Because I've been on so many sets designed to mimic such industrial spaces ("there is an endless demand for porn involving having sex in such masculine work places—oil refineries, space port mechanical bays...something about raw industrial spaces makes men think a lot about fucking other men while they are working" my agent once told me), every time I'm in one like this, I get a bit aroused.

We move through another door and into a larger space with a huge sliding door to one side. The door we've come out of says "MEN." Another identical one across the room says "WOMEN." The huge sliding door says "TRAM."

"Where are we now?" I ask.

"Almost there," Sylas says.

Though I know I should feel in danger, for some reason, I don't. Some suicidal impulse, maybe? I don't feel any threat.

The tram door slides aside and we step out onto a walkway next to a track. When the door slides closed behind us, a message repeated in three different languages reminds us to watch our step, then tells us that the tram is approaching. The difference between the pod that arrives and the pod that had greeted me when I was first picked up what seemed like ages ago is immense. This pod looks as though it's about to fall apart; the glass is fogged over where it isn't cracked, and the carpet is frayed to the point of having holes in it.

Sylas steps on without hesitation, though, and I follow him. When he sits, I have a moment of squeamishness, but then follow suit.

The message tells us in three different languages that our next stop is Core Station.

"Today is your fourth day on the station," Sylas says.

"I guess so," I respond. It's been so overwhelming in so many ways that it has been hard to keep count.

He nods.

"Will this be your first time anyplace below the dome?" Sylas asks. I can tell from his tone he already knows the answer to this.

"Yes," I say. He nods again.

The tram pulls to a stop and we get out. As soon as the doors open the smell hits me. People. A very large number of them. Washed, unwashed, sick, healthy...*people*. The scene is one I'm very familiar with. As a reflex, my hands go in my pockets so that I can feel if someone tries to take my wallet. It's only then that I remember I am not carrying anything. My entire safety and security is in the hands of Sylas.

Sylas reaches over and pulls up the hood on my jumpsuit, then pulls his own up over his head. Immediately the hood tightens itself down and then forms a seal over my mouth and nose. The smells that had almost become mere background to me go away and now all I can smell is plastic and a tiny hint of charcoal. I touch the newly formed mask to find that it has made a grill across the lower part of my face; it is filtering the air as I breathe it in. I look over to see that the same thing has happened with Sylas' suit.

All around us the street is a riot of color and sound. He leads me through alleyways, stepping carefully around groups of people stopped to talk and drink from tiny cups on saucers. Some of them are in jumpsuits like ours, a few with hoods and masks up. Others are barefaced, wearing thick beige cotton clothes and round red hats. No one even bothers to do more than glance at us as we move by.

He takes me around a corner and suddenly the great wall of the station is in front of us. Huge, steel, and curving away into the sky, it gives me a moment of dizziness.

"Try not to look upward too far; it can be very…unpleasant," Sylas says.

We follow along the curve of the wall until we reach a large door. He stops and looks back the way we've come. Then he looks over his shoulder further along the direction we had been going. He pulls aside a small panel beside the door and quickly keys in a sequence. The door slides aside and he motions for me to step in quickly. Once I do, he presses another button and slides the tiny hatch closed. He barely manages to step inside before the larger door shuts. We're in total darkness for a moment, then a series of fluorescent lights flicker on. Just to my left is a hole in the floor and a ladder leading down.

It takes us a long time to get to the bottom. After a few rungs of the ladder, I slide the hood backward. It reclaims the material that had formed a mask, loosens, and slides back over my shoulder. I hear his soles clang on the decking under me and I'm down after a few more rungs. He opens a door similar to the one we entered and we both step through. He closes it behind us.

"We're at the lowest part of the station, now," he says.

Out of instinct, I look up at the ceiling. I imagine I can feel the weight of the entire station pressing down on me. Just beyond where we're standing is a long set of stairs leading down. I remember pictures I've seen of deep underground rail stations from the long ago past. At the bottom of the stairs I can just make out a large airlock-style door.

"What's down there?" I ask.

"Beyond that door lies the jewel of the station," Sylas says. "The yeast farm."

I start down the stairs but he stops me. "That's not on the tour for today. Or ever, really."

"Why not?" I ask.

Again, he cocks his head to the side and sighs. "For one, it takes a while to get through the scrubbing and decontamination routine before going in. We need to get you back soon. For two, yeast likes it when it is very warm and very moist."

I flinch.

"Like so many people, you don't like the word," he says and laughs.

"I never have."

"Imagine, then, being in such a condition. It takes a...special...kind of person to go into that level of humidity unaffected. You...did not strike me as that kind of person," he says and gestures for me to follow him. The entire time, I keep thinking that this is bizarre, and that my trust in this person is even more bizarre. For some reason, though, I trust him.

We walk steadily away from the wall, turning corner after corner. I'm hopelessly lost at this point. Suddenly, we turn a corner and go from bare corridors to a street. He keeps walking.

We turn a corner and I'm hit with it: I've been on this street before. The shops are all weavers. There, near the corner, is the very place Olver bought my jacket.

"I can see you remember," Sylas says. "This street is indeed where he brought you that first day."

"How did you know?" I ask.

"I was there, watching. Many of us were. We were ordered to stay off the streets and vacate the shops, but we have ways of watching if we want to."

"Can we stop in? I'd like to say hello to the person who—"

"She is gone," Sylas says.

"Gone?"

He nods and keeps walking. "She dared to ask for money for the jacket since, as you know, it was a fine piece of work. She protested that she didn't have enough money to feed her family. She closed her shop that evening and the next day it never opened."

"Surely she's just sick or maybe gone on a—"

"A what?" Sylas asks. "A vacation? Do you truly think that anyone who lives here can afford such a thing?"

He leads me through a wall of people and endless processions of food carts for what has to be an hour before eventually coming to a building. Steps lead up to its door. This whole street, now that I raise my head to look at it, is made to resemble something out of the late

20th century back on Earth. Sylas knocks. The door opens a crack and through it I see the glint of a barrel. Then the door closes, I hear the sound of a lock being disengaged and then the door opens all the way this time. I follow Sylas as he steps inside.

My eyes adjust as we follow a woman with a gun down a hallway. Eventually we get to a door and she knocks on it. She says something in a language I don't understand to Sylas and he says, "yes, I think so." She nods in response.

The door opens and I can smell a cat. Inside someone is listening to music—something very old, soft, and sweet. The woman walks past me, eyeballing me the whole time.

Sylas clears his throat and I turn to see he's already inside. I walk in and he closes the door behind me, saying something in a language I don't understand. Down the hall a boy's voice responds in that same language. The music shuts off and I hear the sounds of metal clanking against metal in the kitchen. Sylas gestures for me to move in front of him down the hall.

As soon as we come around the corner it takes everything I can do not to curse. Standing in the kitchen pouring water into the kettle for tea is a boy who looks exactly like Olver. Sylas laughs low in his throat. The boy puts the tea into the kettle and sets it on the burner, flipping the ignite switch.

"Jamie Van Ryan, I would like for you to meet Salil. Salil, this is the man I was telling you about," Sylas says moving past us both through to the other room. Just like Olver, the boy's smile is stunning. But for the boy being about a foot shorter and so skinny it almost hurt to look, they could be twins. "Come," Sylas says from the other room. "There is much to discuss."

In the other room Sylas is sitting on the floor in front of a small

59

wooden table. On it are fruits and nuts in small dishes and three beautiful white porcelain cups with blue dolphins painted on them. Sylas gestures for me to sit next to him. The boy takes the other space.

"Son?" I ask.

Sylas shakes his head. "Clone."

Salil smiles again. "He knows?" I ask.

"It is a fact of which he is quite proud, actually."

We sit in silence for another moment. The kettle whistles and Salil goes to bring the tea back in. He pours for us and the room fills with the smell of dark spice.

"Does…?"

"Does His Highness, the great Olver know? Of course not," Sylas says, barely controlling the contempt in his voice.

"Then…?"

"That is the matter before us today. And I'm afraid that our traveling has taken up so much time, we do not have much left for niceties."

"How old?" I ask.

"Well, when it comes to clones, there is never a direct answer, as you know. Internally, in the matter of his bones and glands, he is fifteen. However, Salil was only decanted a year ago."

I had picked up the tea and was about to sip, but I nearly dropped my cup at this.

"What?" I ask.

"At great cost to our…movement…we have acquired technology that allows us to greatly speed the development of a clone," Sylas says. He sips his tea and nods afterward. It's hard not to see the pride in Salil's face.

"But mental development…?" I'm desperately trying to bring up anything that I can remember about cloning.

"That is part of the technology. Salil is already the mental equal to His Highness, Peace be Unto his Name, The Great Olver." Again, barely contained fury.

"It is wonderful to finally meet you, Mr. Van Ryan," Salil says. "It is my great hope that you will join our cause."

I am dumbstruck. His expression, his word choice…all exactly like the man I'd just left a few hours ago. The only difference was that the voice had not yet fully deepened, and so it took on the hollow buzz of a boy of fifteen usually has on some of the notes.

"And so we come to it," Sylas says. "There are two of them. Salil is the first subject, the test subject to prove that the technology works. He has already played his part in this glorious revolution," Sylas reaches over and grasps Salil's shoulder and it clicks—he's been raising the boy.

"My first son, Faisal, we lost in an early skirmish. The universe has seen fit to grant me another opportunity to raise a child."

Some part of me looks on in jealousy. A clone kid had wound up winning the dad jackpot whereas my own father and I had never once gotten along, let alone any of the other men my mother dragged through the house. This kid popped out of a tank of slime a year ago and was the light of Sylas' heart.

"The other is approaching full adulthood as we speak. Very soon he will be ready for his part in this movement," Sylas says.

"Where did you get the genetic material?" I ask. The tea has finally cooled enough and I sip it, marveling—it is some of the finest tea I have ever tasted in my entire life.

"Suffice it to say that the man has lived alone for quite some time, and that, as you have seen, we have people working inside his mansion," Sylas says with a satisfied air. "It is amazing that, despite his level of power and, admittedly, not inconsiderable charm, he has chosen to remain alone."

"Until now," I say.

"Until now," Sylas says, nodding.

"So," I asked, gulping down more of the tea. "What is the plan?"

# THE PAST

Over the decades, I've gotten used to people seeing me as just my body. It's the business I'm in. They spend their time getting acquainted with how wrists look in restraints, or how I tense my stomach when someone first puts themself inside me. It's a form designed to allow someone to cut me up into individual slices like that. It encourages them to, in fact.

The most intrusive thing, though, is when I meet someone who desperately wants to put the pieces together. After all, people who watch my films see the body I want them to see. Color corrected, laser sculpted, digitally retouched, etc. The guy you see in my vids bears a resemblance to me, sure, but he is a flawless god in the prime of his youth, and I am the pimpled, stubbly, gassy and bloated twin. Most people (and let's be honest, when I say that, I mean "most men" in my case) know this, and they prefer the illusion to the reality. The airbrushed fantasy is what they want.

Back in the early days, though, I did go on a date with one young man who'd been very up front with me about being a fan. Back then, I didn't see anything necessarily wrong with it. He was skinny and young and I thought, what harm could he do? By then, in my off time, I'd become a blue belt in Karate, so I figured I could handle myself.

The date part went well. He wore a tie and a nice jacket. He took me to a nice sushi and Vegan hot dog place. We drank a couple of beers with hops grown on a local floatfarm just off the coast. He asked me back to his place which was nearby, and I said yes.

The sex was okay. A little vanilla, but that's to be expected. After, he got up to go pee and wash off. I touched his bedside wall to call up some music while we cuddled and came down and that's when I saw it. On the open screen was a file marked with my last name. I grinned and, curious to see which film he'd been watching while he touched himself alone, I opened it.

It took me a moment to register what I was seeing. What he'd done was splice together all of the parts of my films where I was fully dressed and not yet engaged in the act with anyone. He'd used some sort of program to model that me, the me that wasn't naked and being pleasured, but instead the me that was dressed and doing things like baking a cake or running the vacuum. He'd spliced them together into this looping reel that made it seem like I was a boyfriend or husband, complete with manipulated dialogue to go with it. Instead of me being his sexual fantasy, something to fulfill a temporary urgent physical need, he'd turned me into a digital relationship where he had complete control of me, the me that looked somewhat similar to the one that I saw in the mirror every day.

Something about it, about how much more intimate that seemed than if he had just been watching me get fucked, sent a shiver through me. When he came out and saw what I was watching, he immediately knew how I felt. He begged me to let him explain but I was already halfway dressed. I was out the door faster than I've ever been in my life. He tried to get on the lift with me, but I stopped him.

When I got back to my place, I checked my requests and immediately booked a photo shoot that would take me off world for a week.

# OLVER

"Remember to inhale deeply once the liquid reaches your nose, my love," Olver said. "It will help you acclimate quickly."

"I remember," I say.

Once more, the cockpit of the mech was filling with the oxygenated liquid that would also connect my mind to the control center of the robot. The liquid moved side to side with the tides that were pushing on the platform on which we all stood that afternoon. I could watch the world outside sway even as the gyroscopes on the legs moved to keep me stable.

This was my fifth time in the mech. Though I told Olver repeatedly that, while I found it interesting, piloting the machine wasn't something that I was excited about, he insisted that we keep doing it. "It is something we can share, my love," he would say. All of that was leading up to this, I think. Across from me, though I couldn't see it yet, stood his own mech—the one he had inherited after his father had passed away. The one that had saved his life.

Once I was connected, we were going to launch into low orbit together.

I would be lying if I said that this idea didn't frighten me.

"But you've done many much more dangerous things, my love," Olver had said.

Not for the first time, I began to wish I could see myself the way he saw me.

Once the pinkish liquid reached my nose, I opened my mouth and inhaled deeply. Even after this many times, my brain still panicked a moment. Then my body calmed down and I could relax my shoulders. Once the liquid covered my eyes, the readouts began to swim before me. I could now see information about the amount of fuel I had, the status of the weapons onboard, and I could see Olver's mech standing across from me on the platform floating on an extended arm of the spire of the station sticking up just above the surface of the world ocean.

"Okay, I'm in," I say.

"Splendid! Consider this, my love; there are people below who live their whole lives without ever seeing the surface of the ocean as you are doing at this very moment," Olver says.

I took a moment to look around. Waves as far as I could see in all directions. That was what I expected. What I didn't expect is that the various sensors of the mech picked up subtle variations of color in them. Purpleish here, reddish there.

"Can they really make the jump to orbit all by themselves? We don't need boosters or anything?" I ask for the tenth time.

"Through a combination of anti-gravity fields and weight dispersion technology, yes. Long gone are the days when someone needed to burn immense amounts of fuel simply to go from the surface of their world into orbit," Olver says.

"I'm not really a pilot," I had protested. He had laughed, "Neither am I, my heart. Thank goodness we are not going to war, but instead on a sight-seeing trip."

"Couldn't we just use your yacht instead?" I had asked. This made him laugh harder.

"While that would certainly provide us with a more comfortable time—the couches are truly excellent on the observation deck, for instance—we would be...*removed*...from the sight. This way, we are connected to it...one with it..." Olver had said and then done something delightfully obscene with his fingers that effectively ended the conversation.

And now here we stood.

"Okay," Olver says, "call up the orbital launch checklist and begin to ask the mainframe to make the checks required, my love," Olver says.

I do. The machine begins to run through the items on the checklist smoothly one after another. The noise increased around me, and I felt a thickening of the liquid. "Right about now," Olver says. "You'll be feeling the liquid in the cockpit become more viscous. This will hold you comfortably in place while the mech accelerates. Once you are in orbit, it will once more relax. Do not be alarmed," Olver says.

The machine informed me that it had finished the checklist and asked me to tell it where I wanted to go. "When it asks you for a destination," Olver says, "tell it the following coordinates." The numbers came across my vision. I told the system that was our destination and it thanked me, then told me to prepare for lift off.

"Let the machine do the work, my heart," Olver says. "Try to relax and enjoy the ride. I will see you in orbit!" With that, his mech rose into the air, paused, then seemed to make itself less man-like and more sleek, then was gone over the horizon. My own machine counted down for me, telling me to relax, as well. The next eight minutes were simultaneously glorious and terrifying. I was jounced around, and the noise, which started far too loud for comfort, became only louder as we went on. I was dimly aware that the surface of the planet-wide ocean of Elgram flashed by below until suddenly it was no longer there, and below was a wash of blue and white. The noise quit so quickly that I thought surely something had gone wrong. The readouts were green across the board, though, and reporting everything in perfectly working order.

Just as the liquid surrounding me grew less thick, Olver's voice greeted me. "There you are, my love," he says. "Welcome to orbit. Or," he adds, and I can hear the quirk of his lips as he teases, "should I say, welcome back to orbit, eh?"

I wanted to say something in return, but I was aware quite suddenly of where I was and the view that had appeared before me. I could see the horizon of the planet and the sun peeking from behind it. Olver had chosen the exact coordinates for us to see what generations of astronauts before us had called orbital sunset. Though I have been in orbit of many worlds, I have never been at the right angle to see it. Yet, here I was, a shell of metal barely an inch thick at its deepest point all that separated me from the vacuum of space, and beyond the danger, the most beautiful sight I had ever seen.

"You don't disappoint, do you?" I say.

"It is my aim to overperform in all things when it comes to you, my heart," Olver whispers in my ear. My readout tells me his mech is just a few feet from me, but I cannot take my eyes off the incredible sunset finishing just before my eyes. "You are now one of only a handful of people who have piloted my mechs into orbit. You are part of my elite inner circle, now, my beloved."

Because I'm linked to the sensors of the mech as if there were my own senses, I feel him take my hand. The system is so sharply attuned, I can feel him gently squeeze. I squeeze back.

There we are, hand in hand, in orbit, as the last rays of the sun peak behind Elgram 34C.

A point comes up on my nav screen. The mech asks if I want to orient toward it. "There, far off in the distant heavens, is your star," Olver says. I tell the system yes. Olver is still holding my hand as we gently turn. "Sol. A middle range yellow star with eight full planets circling it, and one disputed planetoid mass." He laughs. "Consider it. Billions upon billions of people living out their lives with only that one planet to call home for so many thousands of years, and now here we are, you and I, looking at the beginnings of our species as a distant point in a night filled with others just like it. One of billions and billions."

"You're a poet," I say.

"I considered it when I was young. But what is a poet compared to a ruler?" I could hear the distraction in his voice.

Another point showed up swimming before my eyes. Without waiting I tell the system to turn to the new coordinates. Immediately I could see what he was trying to show me—on the opposite side of the planet, the sun seemed to be coming up. In reality, it was our own orbit, spinning so quickly around the equator, that was bringing us back to the sun side faster than the planet below was spinning.

We hold hands as the sun rose over the horizon of the planet to greet us once more. I hear him laughing quietly in my ear. I couldn't help but smile.

"And what is a ruler compared to a star?" Olver asks.

I didn't say anything.

Neither did he.

# LIKE SOMETHING

# FROM A DREAM

Day 125.

"Report Doctor Hewer Room 1011 500 hrs."

At 5 o'clock I am outside the door.

Take off clothes the man says. I do.

Lie down on bed the man says. I do.

There is a time I would have been embarrassed to be the only naked person in a room, especially with females present. Today, things are different.

They remark about how they don't have to shave me. The young woman's hand lingers a bit longer than is necessary. I ignore it.

A man comes in. Gray hair. Hunched. Voice is very calming.

He asks me if I'm comfortable. I think it doesn't matter if I am or not.

What's going to happen is going to happen.

It has to.

Lights lower. There is a hissing sound and a soreness at the back of my neck.

My eyes grow heavy.

When I wake up a tall woman in a lab coat and glasses asks how I feel.

Okay, I say.

The tall woman asks me if I understand.

I do, I say.

Two young women take off restraints and lead me to a room where I put my clothes back on.

I leave.

# THE PAST

"The problem you have, have always had," my friend Aaron says, "is that you're were always stunningly beautiful." He takes a sip of his juice.

We're both sitting in Café 11011 for our weekly juice cleanse.

"I know this stuff is supposed to keep our DNA from sliding around and mutating and all," I say a bit too loud in the direction of the Mixer, "but I wonder if it could actually taste any worse." He doesn't look up but I can tell he's heard.

"Even in the pictures from when you were little I can see it. Huge doe eyes, tiny little shoulders. Hell, I probably would have molested you."

"Gee, thanks," I say and take another sip and roll my eyes.

"I'm just saying—you already had all the qualities that make boys go wild for girls from before you even had any desire to use those qualities to your advantage. It is absolutely no wonder to me, then, that the boys found you early and that here we are, not all that long after, and a company wants you to get naked for them. I say go for it."

"I don't know," I say. I can feel the muscles around my mouth are tensed trying to defend themselves from the assault of how bad this juice tastes. I can see Aaron making the same face.

"I'm jealous, obviously. Still, though, it's a lot of money."

It is a lot of money. He's not wrong there. I don't say that out loud, though.

"Would you do it?" I ask. "I mean, if they asked you. Like right now."

He sips and barely controls his face from shuddering in disgust. "It would depend on the money." I know him enough to know, though, that means yes. "Have they said what they want you to do?"

"At first, they just want me to come in and get scanned. Then they'll send the scan around and see if anyone is interested. They own a whole bunch of companies here and all over the colonies."

"Mars porn," Aaron laughs. The stereotypical image of some yokel in overalls and a cheap, barely functioning oxygen rig comes to mind. Their cocks covered in rich black soil from their giant, dirty farmer hands.

"The guy said, though, that he was pretty sure I'd be working by next week." I finish the last of the bitter clear sludge in one slurp and barely keep back a choke. I shake my head to clear it and set the empty container down with the others to be recycled. "But what about school?"

"Are you kidding," Aaron says. "Who the hell cares about finishing some lousy degree and trying like hell to get a gig doing dentistry on some Jupiter-and-back run cruise liner when you could be making that same amount of money in a few hours for doing what you'd normally do on any given Saturday, anyway?"

# SYLAS

"...Okay, but I'm still unclear. How is it you've disabled the sensors in one of the main rooms in the palace?" I ask.

"The guest room he has put you in isn't one of the main rooms. In fact, it is quite far from what you might call the central area. While it did have security, it had far less than any other room in the entire plan. Initially," Sylas says, "it was designed to be the room where an ambassador could stay. One would think that would be the place where the highest level of surveillance would occur, but his everlasting countenance, may he reign for eternity, had a different plan in mind," Sylas says. "The idea was to leave quite a lot of the normal security procedures conspicuously absent, so that when the ambassador's people scanned the room, they would find nothing amiss. His highness, then, could expect some... relaxation, which could then lead to some slip up in communication. They were thinking much more about watching someone trying to communicate *out*, and not at all about people trying to break their way *in*." Sylas' tone borders on smug, but the satisfaction in it is a turn on. "All we really had to defeat was a perfunctory level of armor and a great deal of fairly low-level audio surveillance. Since there was no ambassador staying in that wing, those machines were not even monitored.

"But how did you know I wouldn't be staying...I dunno...somewhere closer to the heart of the palace. The master chambers, for instance?"

"I have no doubt you would have been moved there eventually. But for now, he wanted you where he could keep you all to himself with as little...shall we say, oversight, as possible. The choice to put you in a room with so few eyes watching was deliberate. We capitalized on that," Sylas says. I can tell he's quite proud of himself.

"So why don't you guys just go in from there? Mount an assault from that room?" I ask.

"As I said, it is a singularity in the palace's security scheme. The second a travel pod moves even an inch from that suite of rooms, the level of security goes up tenfold and increases exponentially from there the closer one gets to the heart of the palace. We are working on getting our people into those key positions, though," Sylas says almost wistfully.

"Tell me the plan again," I say.

"Is it unclear?" Sylas asks.

I don't say anything.

"Are you alright?" Sylas asks.

"Yeah," I say. "I just didn't sleep very well last night."

"Bad dreams?"

"I'm not sure," I say. I sip the tea that we had poured for us. It's strong and good.

"I would think that the bulk of what we have planned would be very clear," Sylas says. "We have cloned his supreme highness and educated that clone to align itself with our goals, ideologically. We will then...replace...one with the other."

The room was silent for a moment. "And what will happen to him, the actual one?"

Sylas glances down at his tea, says nothing. "The question is, are you willing to help us?" he says.

"What if I'm not?" I ask. "What if...what if I go back and report all this?"

"That would be...unfortunate. We have plans in place for such a contingency, though, I assure you," Sylas says without looking up from his cup. I look over at Salil, but his face is just as unreadable. No reactions. It means they've talked about all of this before I arrived—nothing that is happening is in any way a surprise.

"I need time to think," I say.

Sylas shakes his head, "that, unfortunately, I cannot provide you. As they say, this offer is 'time sensitive,'" he says and smirks. His eyes meet mine for the first time in a while. "But I would ask you this: do you truly know him? You have barely met. What do you know about the things he has done?"

I had to admit to myself that I knew nothing, but the idea of saying that made me mad. It felt like saying so was admitting I was stupid or weak.

"I can see you don't want to say because your ego is telling you that would be an admission of weakness," Sylas says. I nod and he smiles in return. "What if I ask you to make no decision for a week, and in that week you allow me to show you what he has done...what life is like for us in the lower levels? Would you at least agree that would be fair?"

I feel like even agreeing to that much was agreeing to the whole thing. What I felt was that I needed to get on the next shuttle off the planet. To warn Olver, to warn the authorities that this was brewing right under their noses and then get the hell out of this system as fast as possible. But there was also something to what Sylas was saying. After all, I had seen things that had unsettled me. I did have a sense that there was more underneath the surface.

# THE PAST

It may sound odd to someone not in the business, this idea of someone buying you for a period of time. Or, I guess I should say, renting.

It's not.

Since there has been the concept of exchange, men have understood that they can give something to someone else in exchange for access to sex. This other person, usually another man, would then allow the first man access to the women, men, or children that had been procured through violence for a specified period of time. Most people are able to understand that fairly easily so long as the period of time is relatively short, usually until the first party ejaculates or thereabouts. Then the access is revoked and the woman, man, or child is recovered and the whole transaction begins again.

But what of this idea of someone selling themselves? Still not that difficult for most people to grasp. The exchange rate might differ, someone believing themselves to be worth more than the standard market rate, usually, but the exchange goes much the same way as before, lasting until the other party (the payee, as it were) finishes what they set about to do.

It is in the idea of a long-term sale or, again, rental, that things begin to get difficult to comprehend. The price usually goes up quite a bit, and there has to be a significant amount of trust involved that the "merchandise" will be returned in relatively the same condition that it was when the purchase occurred, but really the only difference is the amount of time involved. A full day, two weeks at the Cape, a month's excursion to the stations over Io, the terms might differ but the idea is the same. The purchaser or payee is indicating that they want something...well... *more*...from the encounter. Simply getting off on/in/near another human being is not enough. Since the price can and usually does go up so much, these are almost always men of wealth, and often come from families of wealth, which, as you might imagine, can have issues.

The truly long-term sale, though, is something of a rarity. The value involved goes to extremes—either the person being sold is worth so little to the seller that they do not expect the merchandise to come back at all, or the merchandise is worth so much, the price so great, that there is a certainty that at some point the payee, the person paying for the time/attention/access to the body will run out of funds. Those of us who work in the sex industry, if you will pardon, are used to all of these levels (those of us who work in film especially), but it is this highest tier that is reserved for people like...well, to be honest, people like me.

Though rare, the offers do come in. To be fair, they come to me from all of the levels mentioned above, but the offers from this highest tier are not perhaps as rare as you might think. By the time I was able to drink legally on the outbound stations in orbit (who so often clung like barnacles to the oldest of old Earth traditions about things like that), I had already had several offers to come and live the rest of my life in comfort and ease as some old man's plaything. The price in those cases functioning as a kind of dowry, though paid directly to me—the expectation was that I'd marry and become exclusive property.

As you can see, I never accepted these.

Well, at least not while I was still young, and people were still interested in filming me in various ways. I kept telling myself that the offers would still come in once I was old, and no longer wanted to do what I'd been doing.

As I've gotten older, the offers have slowed, though. The eternal youth effect of jetting from world to world faster than light has certainly lengthened my career, but...

And then, one day, a paper envelope arrived. In this day and age, the cost of obtaining an envelope made out of crushed wood pulp alone must have been staggering. In it was more paper with a message in the most beautiful handwriting I'd ever seen (indeed, some of the *only* handwriting I'd ever seen) in actual ink (again, the cost!). It was signed simply "Olver."

# OLVER

I find Olver sitting by one of the large outer windows. On the table is some sort of machine. He's adjusting a set of screws as I sit down across from him.

"Did I wake you, my heart?" he asks.

"No," I say.

Out the window is dark blue as far as I can see, the lights so low that we don't reflect in the glass.

"My father always had trouble sleeping. Even before the war. I would wake up in the middle of the night and he would be in the garage tinkering with the car. It never seemed to make the right noises to his ears," he says. He finishes on those set of screws and begins adjusting another identical set on the other side of the machine. "Working on the machines calmed him."

I pull my knees up into the chair and wrap the robe around me like a blanket.

"After a time, I started trying to make sure I woke up. He thought that I had the same insomnia he had, but I was setting alarms for myself. I liked the quiet of the morning hours where I had him all to myself. Even though we didn't talk. Occasionally he would ask me to hand him a tool. I have never been more proud of any achievement in my life than I was when he would ask for a particular tool and I would know the right one to hand him."

The machine he is working on makes a clicking noise, then a loud snapping noise. He leans back in his chair as a small fan on the front begins to spin, it's tiny whirring seems the only sound for miles.

"What about your mother?" I ask.

Without taking his eyes off the machine he says, "she was a poet. From what people tell me, she was quite a good one, but poetry…poetry doesn't make a lot of sense to me." He leans in and flicks a switch. The fan spins to a stop. "I admire people who can write words in beautiful phrases, but that is a skill which is beyond me." He sets the tool he was working with down. "Why did you awake?"

"Bad dreams," I say. He nods.

"Shall I ring for coffee or tea? Perhaps something stronger?" he asks.

I shake my head no. We both wind up looking out the window into the deep, cold ocean beyond.

Another night, wandering, sleepless.

The lift opens and there I am, standing on the floor of the immense cavern. Against the wall to my right was the enormous doors that lead to the open sea beyond. To my left, the mechs, as Olver called them; a row of giant machines standing upright like soldiers waiting for humans to plug themselves in.

Though their heads are crude likenesses of a face, a large, glaring red all-seeing jewel in the center of their foreheads rather than eyes, there is no escaping the feeling that they are watching me, colossal sentries standing in silent judgment. That somehow they know what it is I'm planning. My footsteps echo, bouncing back from strange angles, making me look over my shoulder to see who is following. It takes what seems like forever to cross the bay to the far said, the door that stands next to another huge hatchway.

I punch in the number that I saw Olver use not so long ago and the door opens. Inside is another chamber, just as tall, but not nearly as long or wide. In it stands only one mech. The door slides closed behind me and for a moment, there is only darkness. Then the lights come up. That's when I see that the cockpit is open, the giant's belly exposed, and that someone is sitting on the lip of the metal plate that should be covering that open belly, their feet dangling off into the air.

"Hello, beloved," Olver says. I jump. His voice echoes through the chamber.

"I was wondering where you were," I lie.

"The rungs on the outside of the leg," he says. I climb up, then use the handhold he points out to swing over to stand next to him in the cockpit of the machine. There is a single chair with metal plates near the foot and handholds near the end of the armrests, but other than that, I see no controls.

"Sit," he says. When I do, the handholds fit naturally in the palms of my hand, and the plates at the foot are exactly where my feet land. He stands back for a moment and shakes his head.

"What?" I ask.

"Almost as if it was made for you," he says, smiling with pride.

"We're just very close to the same size," I say. He flips a switch and the plate he had been standing on closes behind us. Immediately the cockpit is bathed in a gray light that seems to come from everywhere and nowhere at the same time. I'm just about to say something about it when the walls around us disappear and I can see in all directions as if the machine did not exist. I gasp, and Olver laughs.

"Squeeze the left handhold," he says. As I do, the area in front of me comes alive with graphics and information. It's giving me distances, capabilities, statuses; missiles, guns, bombs. It is impossible not to sud-

82

denly feel like a god.

"Powerful, no?" Olver says. I nod. "This one was my father's. Though the ones in the chamber beyond are ten times more powerful, I prefer it."

"How many chambers like that one exist?" I ask. Everywhere I look, the information flows with me. No matter the angle of my neck or set of my eyes, the outside world is broken down into information to be consumed.

Olver kneels down so that our eyes are level, "more and more each day." The gleam in his eyes is intoxicating. He stands and flips the switch and the cockpit fades to become merely a metal chamber and a chair, once more. The front wall of the cockpit slowly falls forward until it becomes again a small shelf to stand on.

Olver pulls me from the chair and kisses me. As we make love there in the heart of the giant robot, I keep thinking about the feeling of having all that power at my fingertips. I'm thinking of that as I finish.

I lean against the pylon and put my hand against the glass. Outside the dome, the water likely moves, dipping and swaying with the current, but there is nothing, no trees or grass or clouds, to show it.

"What are you thinking, dearest one?" Olver asks from behind me.

I start. He laughs a bit. My robe slips open slightly. He steps forward and pulls it tighter around my shoulders. "I'm sorry, my heart, I did not mean to startle you."

"How long have you been standing there?" I ask. I turn back toward the window. In the reflection from the blue light behind us, all I can see are our silhouettes. In the world of the window, I can't see where he ends and I begin.

Olver steps up to me and puts his arms around my waist from behind, then leans his head against my shoulder. "Not long. I just noticed you weren't in bed, so I came looking."

Not for the first time, I notice that he is just a bit bigger than I am, and that something inside me relaxes because of it. I also note how odd this is because I've been with so many men...so many...and some of them with frames far larger than Olver's. Still, something about it being him, just in the short time I've come to know him, changes how I react.

"So?" he asks.

"Mmm?"

"What were you thinking about so deeply while staring out into the abyssal plain?" he asks.

"Do people go diving?" I ask.

"Of course. Once a year, closer to the equator, where there are large coral reefs, there is quite a bit of tourist traffic. They come in from around the territories. There are also a few science stations scattered here and there where people wear special suits to go out and walk along the floor to gather information about...whatever it is they are interested in, I suppose," he laughs.

"Aren't they afraid?" I ask.

"Of?"

"I don't know...animals?" I ask.

"There are a few species that have come back from...what happened..." he says, and I know he means the destruction of his world. "Some of the heartiest of those that did not need to come up to the surface to breathe managed to stay alive and mate and are still around. They tell me that a few of the smaller bottom feeding shellfish are coming back in numbers large enough to count as species, again. You must remember, though, that..." he drifted off. "Well, you must remember that there was a recent change to this world. That more than anything else is what people are here to study."

"But no one from here?" I ask.

"Not officially, no. However, some cobble together suits and go out from the dome. Officially the practice is frowned upon, but unless they have a desire to damage the dome and thereby harm others, my men mostly turn a blind eye." He waited a moment. He gestures toward the window and says, "Would you like to go diving?"

"No," I say.

"Then what else were you thinking about?" he asks.

"That there's nothing to see. No trees or clouds or mountains. I know that the water out there is moving, yet there isn't anything that shows it."

"Yes, there is a current, even this deep. And life, though the largest of the predators only dip down into this zone occasionally. This deep there are only endless valleys that lead to magma vents but even here, this far from our sun, around those tiny cracks, colonies of fairly simple life, but life nonetheless," Olver says. "No matter where you go in the universe, there is always life."

"Now who sounds wistful?" I say.

He hugs me closer. "When I was younger," he says, which I know means before his family was killed, "one of my favorite tutors told me about how, very early on, our species used to think itself alone in all of the universe. All around their world there were examples of how life will always evolve, will always find some way, no matter how precarious, to cling to some tiny source of light and heat in some far flung crevice under tons of pressure and true darkness. Of how, even in the micro-scopic pools of life that existed on a single eyelash, there were species evolved enough to have predator and prey relationships. And yet, in their arrogance, they thought themselves truly unique in a universe so crammed with planets and stars..." He drifted off. "I told him that this couldn't be true...the same species that had become us, the lords of countless worlds, of travel so fast that those worlds could be bounded in a single lifetime...that they couldn't have come from such unmitigated stupidity."

"What did he say?" I ask.

"That it wasn't stupidity, it was fear. Fear that if they weren't unique, then there was no purpose to their existence. He reminded me that it is very easy to be afraid of the depths when standing on the shore. It is only once one dives in, becoming one with the tides and the cycles of life they contain, that fear subsides," Olver says, his voice far away.

"That's beautiful," I say.

"Later that year, we found out that same man was a spy working for a rival family, and he was executed." He kisses me and pulls away. I pull my robe closer around me. "I never forgot what he said, though. Come, let's go back to bed, my heart. They tell me that there is no temperature variation significant enough to feel, but this close to the windows, I always feel that it's a bit colder." He puts his arm around my shoulders and walks me away.

I find him in the hangar again the next night just as I thought I would. I notice an intense blue light surrounding him as I climb up. It dies as I get to the top rung.

"We're going to have to stop meeting like this," I say, pulling myself up the rungs on the leg of the robot.

He smiles, but it doesn't touch his eyes.

"What was that?" I ask.

"What was what?"

"The blue light," I say.

"Ah," he says. "Come here."

I swing over to the cockpit and he takes my hand. He stands up and leads me to the control chair. "Here," he says, taking a silver circlet off his forehead and putting it down over mine. There's a whirring sound as it adjusts to my smaller skull. As soon as it finishes, the cockpit closes just as before, and the walls fade away. Again, I'm staring out into the room around us as though I was simply floating in midair. Information once more hangs before my eyes.

"Now, this," he says, pressing a switch on the top of the left hand controller.

For a second I feel as though I'm falling. The room disappears and becomes a deep sea of blackness. Slowly the blackness fades and I come back to myself, but I feel taller, stronger…a kind of cool lethality seeps into my muscles.

I can't seem him, but I hear Olver say, "The psychic interface system is now engaged."

A pleasant neutral female voice surrounds me, saying, "Welcome to IBIS system 7.3. Initial command?"

"What does that mean?" I ask aloud.

"You and the machine are now one," Olver says.

"Awaiting command," IBIS says.

"This is the true power of this machine. Of course, this one was an early version. The new ones in the bay beyond connect automatically—there aren't even any hand or foot controls, anymore. With this interface," Olver says, "you have but to think a command and the IBIS will do it. For all intents and purposes, it is now your own body."

I look down at my hand and start when I see that the hand of the giant robot has now come up and sits before me mimicking the pose of my own. I flex my fingers and the machine flexes it in perfect sync.

"Ask if for status reports by saying, 'status'" Olver says from somewhere beyond.

"Status?" I ask aloud.

I hear Olver laugh.

"Think the word in your head, that is where she is listening," Olver says.

I think the word, "status," imagining it written in the air before my eyes.

"Status," the voice says, and a list of information swims up to my eyes.

"I'd let you loose to walk around a bit," Olver says from somewhere, "but it takes some getting used to, and there isn't a lot of space in this bay. Tell it 'disconnect.'"

I picture the word typing itself out in front of my eyes and the female voice says, "Disconnecting." I fall back down into the blackness and come back to myself sitting in the chair. I notice the fading remains of a blue light similar to the one I saw surrounding Olver earlier. Once I'm back in my own body, I feel both happy to be myself once more, but also small and frail.

"You'll feel the withdrawal from it for a bit. Try to remember that this is your body, not that," Olver says, pulling the circlet from my head. He sets it on the wall to my left, then pulls me from the chair. The cockpit opens again.

"So?" he asks, taking me by the hand and sitting us both on the lip of the cockpit.

"After everything I've done in the industry, it is unusual for me to experience something new when it comes to my body. This was…new," I say. "You first felt that when you were a teenager?"

"No," he says without moving. "I managed to make the mech move when we were first attacked, but I didn't find out how to connect to it until much later, after the fighting had been going on a while and the soldiers allowed me to join them. That was two, maybe three years later."

"How long did it take you to get over having to disconnect?" I ask.

"You assume that I have," he says and smiles. Again, the smile doesn't touch his face.

He pulls me to him and we make quick, angry love and I can't help what it would feel like if it were happening while I was the connected to the other body I felt I was when I was connected to the machine. I wonder if that's what he's thinking about, too.

I step out of the pool and reach my hand out for one of the servants to bring me the towel he is carrying just as Olver steps through the door into the room. The long traces of light from the bulbs under the water trace lightning bolts across his serene face. He reaches me just as I begin to towel off my shoulders. He steps behind, taking the towel from me, and begins to dry me himself.

"You don't feel any trepidation being naked in front of the servants, my heart?" Olver asks.

"No," I say. "I don't have any trouble being naked in front of anyone," I say.

He continues drying me and I notice that the servants have all left the room. He must have given them some signal.

"I suppose the idea of having a pool when you live at the bottom of the ocean must seem silly," Olver says.

"No," I say. Over us, a projection from the dome outside shows the dark, still deep that surrounds the outside. Olver takes my hand and walks me over to the showerhead. He turns on the water and tests it for a few moments until it's warm. He leads me inside and then steps in, himself. His suit, which likely cost more money than some people in the lower levels make all year, begins to soak as I peel it off of him slowly. "I've been thinking about you all day," Olver says. His kisses are hotter than the water, and he brings me to such a powerful finish that I almost collapse, my legs are so unsteady.

After, we're both laying in one of the many oversize chairs next to the pool, covered in thick, blanket-like towels. With a single word, he lowers the lights. He pulls me closer to him and nuzzles his chin against my forehead.

"I'm curious about something," Olver says.

"What?" I ask.

"Why never any other kinds of movies?"

The chill of the room and the warmth of our huddled cocoon gives me goose bumps.

"What do you mean?" I ask.

"You are very beautiful, you are well-spoken, you could have been in any kind of movie you wanted, but you were never in any other kinds."

"Ah," I say. "Does it bother you that I was never in a romantic comedy? Or an action blockbuster?"

A smile creeps into his voice. "No," he says. "Does it bother you?"

"I never had any desire to be in films like that. To pretend to be something I wasn't. I'm no good at lying," I say.

"Good," he says. "Good," he repeats in a whisper, kissing my forehead.

# LIKE SOMETHING FROM A DREAM

Day 73 of my new life.

Today I learn that I am a weapon.

Today I learn I have been aimed.

"Coach" says this is graduation day.

This is your target "Coach" says. He shows me a picture.

I look at the man in the picture. I don't feel anything for him.

You will kill this man "Coach" says.

I nod.

"Coach" shakes my hand.

Go with these men "Coach" says.

Two men come out of a nearby door. I follow them.

They put me in a van. No windows. We drive for a long time. Then they walk me in to a building through a garage door. It closes behind us.

In the middle of the space is a setup of consoles, cables, monitors, and in the middle of all of it a chair.

"Coach" would make some crack about a dentist if he were here.

I'm told to lie down in the chair.

I'm told to close my eyes and count backward.

Poor bastard I hear one of the men say as I get very sleepy.

What's the cover for this one? Someone else asks.

He's going to think he's an old school porn star. Think the target has bought him another answers.

I'm slipping further under.

Down a long tunnel I hear, did they actually make videos for the target to see?

Yeah, someone else answers. Fakes. We dredge up some old crap off the web, change the face digitally. We have someone inside that's been feeding the fakes directly to "his highness."

Just before I black out I hear standard trigger word wake up kill job. This'll be the fourth one we make this week.

Poor bastard I hear just before I go out.

Which one? Someone asks.

Both someone says

and then blackness.

# THE PAST

"—Some of the ships had his markings on them, some had hers, but you see, the problem was that, both being from the same royal house, the markings were similar colors and had similar shapes. Now add that to the confusion of battle at 1/3 light speed and it was a mess—," he says. He's got the whole camera and lighting crew fascinated.

Something most people don't realize is that almost everyone on a gay porn set is straight. The lighting guys, the sound guys, the camera crew…all of them just waiting for you to shoot your load on the other guy's face so they can take five to call home to their wives and find out what is for dinner.

The ace fighter pilot is straight, too. This happens a lot, as well. Especially after they get discharged from the war. They go do their 4 years, get their clean service discharge, and come back to their home system to find that there is no work for them. Their friends are all too busy with the families they've started raising and the businesses they've taken over from their fathers. Someone has to explain to these guys yet again the time dilation effect; even at the extreme speeds we can zip around the galaxy these days, while they were gone 4 years from their perspective, their planetbound friends (and girlfriends) have lived 20 years or so. They come home somewhat less fresh-faced boys to find a universe that they are no longer in step with. It isn't long before they discover, though, that there are a few industries that are always welcoming of new, young bodies.

So, of course, I run into a lot of them. Always the same—tops that act super butch around the crew (most of whom are likely drone jockeys back from the war themselves), but when it comes time for a scene you can see the hurt in their eyes if you look close enough. Usually being under them, I've gotten very good at seeing it. On some level, having another man accept them, physically love them, even if it is an illusion, is healing.

They are wanted by someone, at least.

The money shot as therapy.

"—So I juke in on his six and I'm dug in. I mean I'm not letting this asshole go. All of a sudden, Nelson says, 'hey, where'd Jackson go?' and someone comes back over the speaker, 'Who?' because, remember, we're all supposed to be using our codenames over open channels. It's the first time, though, so Nelson can't remember Jackson's codename and then there's just this silence when the screen shows scrub one. Nelson was trying to remember Jackson's codename and one of the bogies got in behind him and laid him out—,"

"Back to set!" the guy who is assisting the director says. We're all pretty sure he's a defunct android who has been reprogrammed, but we're all too polite to say anything.

Captain Space Ace rolls his eyes like getting off is the last thing he wants to do, adjusts his robe and comes back over to the bed. His slippers slap the metal floor with each step. Each of those steps might as well be a doorway he passes through, though. His shoulders tense up, his breathing goes shallow. The big bragging man from seconds ago disappears and the lost kid from some outer system comes walking back over.

"Places!" the assistant says.

"Hey," the guy says, letting his robe fall. His eyes catch mine. He's looking for some sign that I like his body, that he's somehow accepted by me.

"Hi," I say. I'm not some antisocial, you know. If it'll make the scene go easier, I don't mind giving the guy a boost. "Wow, you look really great," I say and put my hand on his cock.

Just like that, some small bit of the confidence that he had just a second ago comes back to his eyes, his shoulders, and I think, good— we can probably wrap before lunch.

# SYLAS

When I see the mask lying on the bed, I put it on immediately. The mask means Sylas and I no longer even question whether or not I want to go. Within minutes the side panel opens and I follow him into the night.

As always, we reach another door and as soon as it opens, we take off our masks. He closes the door behind us and I see that we are in an empty section of the station alone. Around us the walls are unfinished, the circuitry exposed, and the debris of construction. Across from us is a large circular hatch.

"Where are we?" I ask.

He grins. "At one time, Olver, long may he reign," Sylas says, the venom dripping from his words, "thought perhaps we might create an economy of tourism. Before anyone could convince him that no one would come to the outer edge of space to look out into an abyss, he began construction on several of these observation areas. He thought that because we, too, have an abundance of water, we might rival the likes of Molokai station out near Stumbough 84 Alpha, or even Reno station around ULAS +25."

With that, he flips a switch and the hatch I'd seen slides aside revealing an enormous window out into the depths. I can tell he wants this to be special and powerful, but it's similar to the windows back in the palace. I act amazed, gaping in wonder. I owe him that much. He leans in close to me almost exactly the way Olver does.

"But, wait…I've been to Molokai. They had observation ports like this every five feet everywhere, but they also had…y'know…fish."

"And so you see the problem. Though we, too, have organisms swimming about, they are nowhere near as abundant nor as…colorful…as Molokaian sealife," Sylas says. "What we have is endless black water. A deep abyss to stare out into."

"Where are we…?" I start to ask.

"In regards to the surface? We're near the bottom of the station, here, just up from the yeast farms. If you could somehow look straight down, you could almost make out the sea bed from where we are, as though you were at the top of a very tall building on Earth."

We both get caught up staring out into the depths. It doesn't take long for a kind of existential cold to creep over me in a way it doesn't back in the palace.

I inhale and then exhale. "At this depth, how long?"

"You would be crushed almost instantly," Silas says.

"How did you know that was what I was going to ask?"

"Because, at this depth, that is the only question anyone has on their mind."

After a moment he goes on. "Interestingly enough, though, we could pressurize you to the same level. Using different gasses or a liquid air supply of some sort. Such things are theoretically possible." I don't say anything about the system the mech used. "If we did that, you could actually go out for a swim without any ill effects. From the pressure, anyway. Then, it would only be the cold of the water that would kill you." Another moment of quiet, then he says, "so many people think of a desert as the most harsh environment in which to attempt survival. This is almost more cruel. 'Water, Water everywhere, but not a drop to drink.'"

"What was that?" I ask.

"A poem from the long ago. The very thing that gave life to us on our homeworld can be the most deadly thing, as well." He goes quiet. It's a quiet I know very well. Have known my whole life.

"You want something," I say.

He nods.

"Then say it," I say.

"He has shown you the suits," Sylas says. I nod. "Shown you what they can do." I nod again. "Shown you where they are stored."

It hits me. "You want them."

He nods this time. "Of course we do."

"To take over the station," I say. He doesn't move. Again, the waiting. "I need to think about that."

He closes his eyes, reaches out, and takes my hand. "What is there to think about?" he whispers. When I don't say anything, he asks, "Has he told you why he wants them? Why he's building new ones?"

"New ones?" I ask.

"The ones that you have been shown, they aren't relics from some long ago army, are they?"

"I don't understand."

"He's been building new ones. For quite some time now, in fact. He's building a new mech army. Did you not ask yourself what for?" Sylas asks. "If he is loyal to the Earth government, then why?"

"He could be trying to sell them," I say.

Sylas shakes his head and squeezes my hand. "You know better than that."

"Look, he's…he's not like you think," I say.

"I know him far better than you do."

"But you...you don't..."

He shakes his head again. I pull my hand away.

"Okay, then why?" I ask.

Sylas stares at me for a moment. "What wouldn't a son do to avenge his fallen father?"

"You think he's going to try to..."

He nods.

"But this is...this is a..."

"Tiny colony on the very back end of nowhere? Yes, it is. Who could possibly suspect it?"

"But that is what I mean," I say. "He couldn't get within lightyears of Earth with a load of weapons like that."

"Not without help, no." He is quiet for a moment, then looks at the display on his wrist. Before I can ask anything further he says, "Come; we should get you back." With a flip of the switch, the hatch slides closed and Sylas leads me through the darkness.

Days later.

"Come, quickly," Sylas says as the doors to the lift slide open. He turns his back and walks away. I stride quickly to follow. We move through the maze of tunnels that I have almost memorized by now. I know that I have to stay quiet through this section. Once we pass a particular junction, I know that the tunnel will straighten out and we will be far enough outside the palace network that Sylas will feel safe talking.

As we pass that very junction, I ask, "where are we going today?"

"To meet Falma," he says. Today, his pace does not slow as much as it has before.

We reach the hatchway that opens to the large market place and go through. Today the market is quieter than it has been in the past. I am trying to figure out why when I notice that the lights are lower than they usually are. "Why is it darker today?" I ask.

"There has been…an incident."

"What happened?"

"Wait," he says over his shoulder. "All will be made clear."

He stops at the edge of a roadway. A small pod comes to a stop near us and the doors beetle open. "In," he says. I climb in and barely get my belt clipped before we're moving. Sylas takes manual control of the pod, something I rarely see, and steers it along a network of smaller and smaller roads until we reach one that goes only one way and is barely wide enough for the pod. If I were to slide the window down, I could easily take a fruit from the stand we pass without flexing my elbow.

Sylas stops the pod and presses the brake. The doors rise above us and we both step out. He touches the surface on a particular spot and the doors slide down once more, the windows grow solid and the skin of the entire pod goes dark. He pockets the key and gestures for me to follow him up a short flight of steps to a front door. The neighborhood is the same. In the oldest livable part of the dome, the deepest part of the structure. Where no one who had a choice would ever choose to live.

The door opens and a little girl with dark wavy hair and brown eyes peers up at us from the gloom inside. Someone asks something in a language I don't understand. The little girl says something, then Sylas says something back in a soothing voice. He gestures to me, then himself, and then to the house. A plump woman with a complicated braid in her hair and white towel in her hand comes to the door behind the little girl. She smiles, but her eyes watch me. Sylas gestures to me and then himself again and says something that includes our names. The woman nods and herds the little girl away from the door. She then turns and walks away, too. Sylas gestures for me to go in. I hear him follow behind me and close the door after himself.

Again, a small room. Again, a small table. Again, the spiced tea wafting around us. The woman sits on one of the cushions with her back to the door. We sit across from her. She says a few things to the hallways behind us and I hear the sound of feet moving in all different directions. "There," the woman says with a sigh. "That should keep them busy enough to not eavesdrop for a bit."

"Falma," Sylas says with a slight bow of his head.

"Sylas," she says, returning the same gesture.

"This is—" Sylas begins to say.

"I know who he is," Falma says. She pours tea and offers the cup to me. Then she pours for Sylas. Then she takes one for herself. Sylas helps himself to some of what looks like honey.

"Yes, outrageously expensive because we can't get them to thrive down here. No matter what we do, it's as if they know they are already drowning," Falma says as if reading my mind. "Still, there is no excuse for not having honey on hand for tea when a guest comes by."

"We don't have a great deal of time," Sylas says. "Tell him what you know."

She nods more to herself than anyone in the room and then says, "Last year, when it began to look like we weren't going to make our quotas, things became very bad." She stirs her tea a bit, then says, "His highness," as if she's spitting. "He said that there would be no repercussions as long as we could make up the differences in the production by a date that was ridiculous. We all knew there was no way we could make it. He knew it, too. So, when we again fell short of even the new date, he accused us of trying to sabotage him. Of trying to hurt him personally.

He said that he suspected what we needed was motivation. That was when he started taking people off the streets."

I look at Sylas. He nods.

"At first, because it was just a person here, a person there, we didn't know if we should believe or not. That's the way of things with people, isn't it? We always think that extreme behavior is a…mistake…something that surely must be a misunderstanding. But it isn't. For so many, the extreme behavior is the normal behavior." She sips her tea and, as a good guest, I take my first sip, too. The tea is bad and the honey doesn't help. I imagine it's the very best that she can afford, though. I make a small noise of enjoyment to show my appreciation. "I was unsure myself until one afternoon I came home to find that no one had been home. Aleer should have been," she said and stopped. For a moment, it was as if she was frozen. "It was a rare day that I wouldn't come home to find him already curled on his bed programming his games. He loved making things to challenge the mind." She taps her temple and smiles. The smile fades quickly, though. "Three days pass. Four. He doesn't come home. No one has seen him. There is no sign of him anywhere. Once we begin to talk, though, it becomes clear. At least one person from every family of a factory worker has simply vanished," she says. "One minute here, the next…" she fades off, shaking her head. "Ten he is. Ten. Adult men have taken a ten year old boy off the very streets he has lived on since he was born."

"Where is he now?" I ask.

She simply stares at me.

"We tried so hard to make the quota, but it was an impossible number. And once we missed the deadline for that one, the deadline for the next was upon us. We could never catch up. For each week we did not make the number, we were told one of our family would be killed. Of course, his highness," again, the venom is powerful, "did not tell us this. This came from his people. He was the shining leader we had all hoped for, still, at least in the eyes of the news stories. What happened to my boy...my beautiful boy...that was never in any news dispatch, never covered on any early evening broadcast. He was here, then he was not."

"He was killed?" I whisper.

"She doesn't know," Sylas says. "What they neglected to tell anyone was that those who were taken would never be returned, even if they were..." Sylas trails off. "To this day, almost no one has any idea where the ones who were taken are, including her."

"Ten he was. Only ten," she whispers.

Sylas leans forward and puts his hand on her shoulder. "You will see Olver hang from the highest pillar I can find."

She nods. I can see that the thought of such violence truly does make her feel better.

I picture for a second the body that I have come to know so well slowly swinging by its neck from a streetlight. I have to get up and leave. I mutter apologies on my way out. I make it to the curb before I throw up.

The hatch slides closed. Sylas has followed me all the way back through the route we took to get here without saying anything. Once we're alone together in the silence of the tunnel, the thought of going back to the palace looms enormous. I feel as if I must make a decision before I can go, but I can't get myself calm enough to even think of what the decision is.

"Why did you show this to me? Why today?" I ask.

"I moved too quickly before. I thought you'd have seen it for yourself, but you didn't. If..." he starts to say but sighs. He blinks, then looks at the floor. "If I'm going to ask you to help us, then I can't give you a reason," he says. "I see that now. You need to have your own reason. So, I'm going to show you."

"I'm not stupid," I say.

He looks back at me. "I never once said or thought that you were. But I can see that this is not who you are."

"What is that supposed to mean?" I ask.

He starts walking back through the maze of tunnels. I follow him. "You aren't a revolutionary. It isn't in you."

"I can fight just as well as anyone else," I say.

"Of that, I have no doubt," he says. "But fighting isn't your first instinct. You've never had to."

I want to say something back to this, but I don't have anything *to* say.

"Don't worry, there is still time. We will teach you," he says.


A long week later.

I'm taken through a labyrinth of service tunnels and maintenance sections to a hatch. When it opens, it is an empty street that I recognize from before. The young man who came to get me leads me to an empty house. Sylas is waiting inside.

"Where have you been?" I ask.

"Am I to be at your beck and call?" he smirks.

"I...wanted to see you."

"And I you, but there have been matters to attend to."

"Such as?" I ask.

He laughs and shakes his head.

"There have been three 'free and fair elections' in the last decade. I suppose that we should be grateful that every time he does not say he won by one hundred percent of the vote. Still, in the end, good men and women, people who truly have vision for how this community could move forward, make something of ourselves…in the end we watch as they make their speech conceding the loss, all of us, including them, knowing that this has all been a false exercise, and then we never hear from them again."

"How do you know, though, that these are faked? Perhaps people truly do just believe in Olver's vision…" I say.

Sylas shakes his head and sighs. "We do not have the luxury of informal polling, but instead whispers in the dark. The effect is the same, though. I talk to enough people. I know what the numbers should have at least been close to."

"You're that connected?" I ask. Sylas doesn't say anything. "Why haven't you run, then? If you think he's this corrupt, you know about his tactics, you could be the one who…" I say.

He shakes his head. "The people who would support me often end up missing. There are eyes and ears everywhere."

"I don't understand…"

"They disappear," Sylas says. "Someone makes a joke about Olver or someone says something about the working conditions and then they are gone."

"But that's impossible. It's a small station, there must be…"

"What?" Sylas says. "Some logical explanation? They ran away? I'm not talking about a few people a decade. At its worst, when we were promised elections two years ago? It was five or six a day."

"But then how could…" I start to ask.

"How could the work population stay the same? Sometimes new people show up. Other times we are told to celebrate! We have gotten a promotion. This almost always means that we have to take over the responsibilities of the person who has disappeared. They invent a new job title for us, but there is no more money for the increase in duties."

"You could refuse the…" I start to say.

"The ones who refuse to take up the slack then disappear, themselves," Sylas says. "They clock out that day and then never make it home."

I shake my head but can't think of anything to say.

"Let's say you're right, that he is…that he is disappearing all these people. If everyone knows, why hasn't anyone contacted anyone?" I ask.

"Contacted anyone like whom?" he asks in return, tilting his head to the side. I can hear the sarcasm in the proper grammar use.

"Colonial authorities. I mean, even…" then it hits me. "Oh," I say.

He nods. "Now you understand. Once we broke that chain of oppression, we also made ourselves answerable to no one but ourselves. And Olver has the thugs, the weapons."

"But, I mean…if this is what is happening, then if all of you rose up as one, surely you'd outnumber his…his army."

Sylas puts his hand on top of mine. I feel how hard the callouses are, the sandpaper grit of them, and I almost curl my thumb over his by instinct, but then jerk my hand away. He looks down and smiles, then shakes his head and looks back at me. "One would think, would they not? The problem is this: people will cling to any tiny scrap of normalcy they can rather than have to fight for something new."

"That's not true," I say.

"It is. Our greatest enemy, those of us who have lost, is not Olver's thugs, or his secret police. No, our greatest enemy is those who have not yet lost anything. The ones whose greatest desire is to wake up tomorrow and not have to deal with change. There are none so blind as those who will not see, yes? Will not—not can not, or simply have not, but those who refuse to see. In order to hang on to their tiny scrap of whatever, they are willing to sell the rest of us out. So we cry 'help us!' in the streets and they close their curtains."

"You've tried," I whisper.

He nods, "and time and time again watch as our men and women and children are rounded up and disappeared for daring to try to stop this…this circle of thieves who rule not by right, but by fear and complacency."

"Olver," I whisper.

He puts his hand on top of mine again. This time I don't move it. "Olver," he says with finality. He makes a gesture and the young man comes in. "Ask youself—why does he make such a huge army of mobile armor suits."

Before I can say anything, the young man ushers me away back toward the palace.

●

Olver and I are alone again in the hangar bay.

"Okay, so why?" I ask. He's installing a new component on his old mech, and I'm watching the readouts on the system scanner, calling off numbers to him when he asks.

"Why what, beloved?" Olver gunts without looking up. At that moment, he's using what seems to be his whole arm strength to wrench something into place.

"Why build this huge army of mechs?" I ask.

He continues pushing for another moment, then relaxes with a sigh. He picks up the towel next to him and wipes his forehead, then stares at me. "If they ever come back, I will be ready."

"Do you think they will?" I ask.

He looks off into the distance. "If they do, I will be ready." He goes back to the wrench, this time straining so hard it looks like his neck will pop. "Where is this coming from?" he grunts.

"Hmm?"

There is a clicking sound and he relaxes, regular color returning to his cheeks. He pants for a moment, then sets the wrench aside. "This line of questions. Where is it coming from?" he asks, looking at me. He picks up the towel and beings cleaning his hands. On the screen in front of me, the numbers all reduce from red to green, and the machine's angry messages stop.

"I was just wondering. I mean, you're at peace with Earth, right?"

He swings his legs out from the open panel and climbs down the ladder. "We were supposedly at peace with them at the time they came to destroy this world, too." He presses a button at the bottom of the leg and the panel he'd been working on closes, then he walks over to me. "What I've learned over time from watching them is this: you cannot trust what they say. As someone once said, 'watch their hands, not their mouths.'"

"And what do you see? When you do that, I mean. When you watch their mouths?"

"That the people of Earth are some of the most vicious, blood-thirsty, power-mad monsters the universe has ever produced," As he's saying this, Olver pulls me to my feet and kisses my hands. "This is why I knew I had to get you away from them."

"Was that your goal?" I ask.

He nods earnestly. "But...I mean...they'll...don't you think they will revolt?"

"There will be some who do not see," Olver says. "There always are.

But over time…over time they will come to understand." He opens the container and pulls out a cigar. For a second, I think he might actually light it, but he doesn't. He puts it between his lips and looks up at the mech's face. The underside of the lid has a golden plate. There are words carved on it, but I can't see what they are. "They'll come to see that what I'm doing is for the best. They'll have to make sacrifices, of course, but those sacrifices will make for a better world for their children's children. One day this world will go from being a tiny outpost on the edges of the universe to the center of power."

The look in his eyes is so distant that for a second, I want to see what he is seeing.

"Of course, as you asked, there will be those who call me mad," Olver says. His eyes focus in on me. Gooseflesh runs down my back. I look away. "What about you—do you think me mad?" He pulls the cigar out of his mouth.

He pulls me closer and kisses my neck. Then he pulls me around in front of him and kisses the top of my spine at the base of my skull, and my mind disappears.

"Where are we?" I ask once Sylas has pulled off my hood. "Why was that necessary?"

Sylas doesn't answer. Instead, he gestures for me to follow him further down the empty corridor, both our steps ringing hollow on the bare metal. The unfinished corridor is lit only every thirty feet or so by a single fluorescent bulb. We cast long shadows onto exposed wires and conduits. Eventually we reach a juncture where the corridor splits left and right. To the left the hallway grows markedly colder. To the right it heats up. He takes us to the left and almost immediately up a set of steps that aren't completely finished. At the top he turns and helps me up.

The room I step into is just as unfinished as the hallway, but at the top is a huge dome of glass. I walk to it while Sylas stays behind me.

"Why are there so many places on the station that are unfinished?" I ask.

"Some are merely plots and plans and schemes that were abandoned over time," Sylas says. "Others are damages that were never repaired. Simply closed off and left to rot."

"Why do you know so many of these places?" I ask.

"These are the places where we meet. Where messages are exchanged. Whispers collected."

I laugh. "I thought I was leaving all of that behind this last time."

He steps up next to me. There is very little light, so almost no reflection of us appears in the glass. "What do you mean?"

"Just before I left this last time, there was an election. The man who won is horrible. Almost immediately he started to put all these plans into place to crack down on the people. Control them. Restrict their crossing of borders."

"We hadn't gotten word that something like that had occurred," Sylas says. "Disturbing."

"You will," I whisper. "It made me happy to be leaving. To think that I might not be coming back this time."

"This time?" Sylas asks. "So it's true? This is not the first time you've made…arrangements…like this?"

I shake my head but don't say anything.

"Why?" Sylas asks.

"Why…?"

"Why have you tried to leave Earth behind so many times?"

"Because it's a shithole," I say. "I hate it there."

Now Sylas shakes his head. "What?" I ask.

"To us, here, the word Earth is blue skies, wind, rain. Actual oceans filled with life." His voice grows distant as he talks.

"Earth is people constantly all over you, wanting things, needing. Police always watching you for any signs of deviation from the norm. It's people always wanting you to follow the rules of their religion even if you don't belong to it."

"You have been harassed in this way?" Sylas asks.

"Yes," I say. "Well, no. I mean, I could have been. It's…complicated."

"Teach me," he says, turning to me and resting his shoulder against the wall.

"Back there, I have a lot of money. Not a lot of status," I say, "but enough money that I can work around whatever rules and laws they make. For the last, I don't know, twenty years or so, though, there's been this…revival. People feeling the emptiness of life and instead of just accepting it and trying to fill it with something good that they make or do, they turn to religion for the answers."

"What is wrong with religion?" Sylas asks. I had never considered that he might have one until just that moment.

"I don't know," I say.

"No, you do, but you worry that I will take offense to whatever you might have to say about it. Don't worry."

"I've been told that before, usually just before someone started screaming at me and then walking out of my life forever. Back when I let people in that close, I mean," I say.

"Try me," Sylas says.

"Last time I left was a while back. The guy just wanted someone to live with him until he passed away. His family had all been killed and he had no one else to see to him as he made his transition. Little to no sex involved, just companionship for someone who was very old and scared of what was coming next. So I went to him, stayed with him for about five years or so, Earth time. He had this wonderful relationship with the idea of passing that wasn't about some passage in some book somewhere. We spent long hours just holding hands and talking about the weather that day. The colony he was on had just achieved balance in the last year or so. He was one of the founder's children, so he was very proud of what they'd accomplished. At any rate, once he was done, I packed and flew back to Earth. From my point of view, I'd only been away five or six years, but Earth time it was closer to ten. Long enough that culture had made a pretty big shift," I say. I lean against the wall, now, too, just like Sylas. "There'd been a rise in religious fundamentalism, and there were starting to be crackdowns on things that gave people comfort. Especially in my industry. Though, to be fair, I hadn't done any films in a while. Still, the companies that had evolved from the companies that I had worked for were experiencing backlash and some were even raided. It was all under the leadership of this man who came to power. I feel like..."

"Like what?" Sylas asks.

"I feel like maybe there is this huge cycle. Like a pendulum, maybe. It swings and swings and when it gets to the extreme of one side, it starts swinging back to the other." I started to move my hand like it was swinging slowly. "People being okay with who they are and with one another and relaxing all the rules," when my hand got to a certain point, I stopped it as if it had reached its apex, then slowly moved it back the other direction, "people getting afraid of how comfortable they have become and seeking some kind of structure, so they reinforce the rules."

"We agree on that. The difference is that this man on Earth sounds like he is...or was, since it has taken you some time to get here...just starting to crack down on the people. With Olver, it is different." It's hard not to feel as if the room just got even colder. "As I've told you, he has made people disappear. He has extorted and lied and..." Sylas realizes how loud his voice is getting and stops himself. He takes a breath. "And that is why you are a gift sent to us."

We are both quiet for a moment. "What if I were to say no? To not help you?" I ask.

He sighs. "Even after all you've heard, could you still say no?"

I don't have an answer for him.


Days later, I am again brought through the tunnels and hatches as always. This time, though, I can sense that we're moving in a different direction. Someplace I haven't seen before. When I emerge, there is Sylas and a guard.

"Come," he says, "I have something momentous to show you."

He walks us through several hatches and down a few long abandoned corridors, judging from the dust and webs.

The last door opens and we step inside. I can hear that the room is enormous.

The lights come up and there, in the center of the room, like some sort of art installation, is a cylindrical tank filled with light blue liquid. In the tube is Olver. Not quite the Olver I know; this one is younger, thinner, his face less filled out, but unmistakably him.

I walk over to it. I hesitate as I do, though, worried he might open those eyes, that somehow, this is the real Olver and that this is some kind of trap.

I hear the door slide closed behind me. "You can go closer," Sylas says.

Because of the low lighting, I see my reflection overlaid onto this clone's face. I put my hand on the tank and then pull back; it's very warm.

"37 degrees Celsius," Sylas says. He steps up to my left. I see both of our faces reflected onto the clone's. "If he'd ever had a mother, this would be the mimic of his mother's womb." I put my hand back on the tube.

"How long?" I ask.

"Any time now, they tell me," Sylas says. "We are just about ready for the plan to move forward."

I notice the clone's eyes twitching. "Is it...is he...dreaming?"

"We think so. Those who created the technology say that they are uncertain as to whether or not dreaming takes place, but centuries of literature say that babies in the womb do, so there's no reason to think that he isn't."

"Will...will he have Olver's memories?"

"No. Even with this level of technology, there is no way to do that. No, if he were going to actually be alive to rule, then we would need to educate him just like anyone else," Sylas says, idly checking readouts on a set of screens next to the tube.

"Alive...what do you mean? Isn't that the plan?"

"No," Sylas says, turning his attention back to me. "No, the idea is that we take Olver, put this clone in his place so that people can see a warm body for a day or so, then we manufacture a change of power."

"And Olver?" I ask.

Sylas stares at me for a moment. "That will depend on what he does once we have him." The clone's arms twitch, almost as if it somehow knows we're talking about it. "There is something of a divide in the council. Some want to simply dump him out an airlock and have done with it. Others wish to torture him for a time as revenge."

"And you?" I ask.

"I want what I think you want…for him to agree to what we've done and leave quietly."

"Will you let him?" I ask.

Sylas sighs. "If he cooperates, if I think he sees the logic of that option, I think I can get the council to agree. If not…"

"What happens to the clone once the transfer of power is accomplished?" I ask.

"We will terminate it," Sylas says. "Quietly, somewhere offstage. 'Former President Olver leaves colony in disgrace' and then we move on."

"With you as President?" I ask.

"There are some who have suggested it. I…I am unsure."

I turn to him. "Why unsure?"

"That is a conversation for another time, perhaps. We should go; you'll be missed," Sylas says.

I take one look back at the doors as the lights go out. Again, I'm scared that those eyes might snap open.

The next day I am brought through the maze of tunnels and hatches to an opening near a street. It is still jarring to me, coming out of the cold, dark world of technology and onto a street that could be in the suburbs of any major city back on Earth. We walk to the back gate of a house, through it, and then through the sliding glass door of a house which is empty.

"Where are we?" I ask Sylas as he walks in from the hallway.

He cocks his head to the side. "Do you believe in our cause?"

"What do you mean?" I ask.

"Our goal. The freeing of our people. Do you believe?"

"I'm learning," I say.

"Meaning you have doubts," he says.

"Is that not okay? Are we not allowed to have doubts?"

Sylas moves closer. "What is it you wish to ask?"

"Okay," I say. "As I asked before, will you take power once...he...is out?" Some part of me feels that if I mention Olver's name, he'll know everything.

"Yes," Sylas says.

"And you don't feel that this rebellion is a little self-serving, then?" I ask.

"I did not decide this, it was decided today," Sylas says. "Why—do you want the power?" he asks.

I sense danger in the answer, so I don't say anything for a moment. "Of course I don't."

"Then who would you rather?" he asks. Again, I sense danger.

"Whoa," I say. "Where is all this anger, this distrust...where is it coming from?"

"Who is this?" Sylas asks, putting a data PAD on the counter between us. On it is a face I haven't seen in a long time.

"Where did you get that?" I ask.

"Who is that?" Sylas asks.

"It's...it's me," I say. On the PAD is a picture of me before the surgeons changed my nose, my skin tone, my cheeks. Before I became Jamie Van Ryan.

"I see," Sylas says. I can tell he already knew, though. He knew before he even asked.

"Does it make a difference?" I ask.

"It very well may, yes."

"How?" I ask. "The person underneath that face is the same person who is underneath this one."

He shakes his head. "The perception is what is key. And the perception is that you have lied."

"There was a fire," I say. "I was very badly burned. It was a long time ago, and I don't talk about it with anyone, really. How is that a lie?" I ask, gesturing toward the PAD.

"You have to remember," he says. "These are not complicated people. They have been kept poor and uneducated by Olver. They don't understand such things. Or, rather, they don't understand why someone would *do* such a thing, unless it was to conceal something."

"So what does this mean?" I ask.

He shakes his head again and looks at the floor. "I don't know," he says. "How old are you, really?"

"Time dilation…"

"Don't quote physics textbooks to me. How old are you?" Sylas asks, emphasizing each word.

"I don't know how you want me to answer that question," I say. "I stopped celebrating birthdays a long time ago."

"The person sitting in front of me appears to be in his early twenties. You give the impression of a boy who is not yet a man but soon will be. But that isn't the case, is it?"

"Does that matter?" I ask.

"It will. To them," Sylas says, gesturing out the window. "They are a beautiful culture, older than even they know. Their traditions stretch back to long before they came to this planet, even if they don't know that, either. But because they have been kept away from the rest of the universe, there are many things that don't come up in their day to day lives."

"You are that certain the old pictures will somehow show up?" I ask.

"If I can find them…" Sylas says, but doesn't finish.

"If I still celebrated birthdays, in a few months I would be turning sixty-two."

Sylas sighs.

"Was a different face, one that you knew was mine before you even asked…was that truly enough to shake your confidence in me?" I ask. Sylas doesn't say anything.

"And now?" I ask.

"We shall see," he sighs. "We shall see."

# THE PAST

It was my agent who gave me the ticket.

"Listen, this is supposed to be the hottest thing around," he said.

We were sitting in my newest apartment. Before the first trip away. I was waiting for the microdermabrasion guy to come over and erase all sense that I had body hair or moles or, indeed, even pores. "He needs to make you look like you're part seal," my agent had said.

He was paying for the whole thing, so I didn't care.

But he wasn't talking about the sandblasting and chemical peeling of my skin. He was, instead, talking about the ticket.

"They called us, too. Remember that. When they call you, you can ask for whatever you want, money-wise," he said. I laughed.

"Okay," I said. "Run it by me again."

"So they strap you into this chair and through deep hypnosis and gently injected chemicals, they convince your body that you've been on a long and luxurious vacation. Fifteen minutes in the chair is the same as taking two weeks in Ibiza, they say."

"You sound like you're reading straight off their promotional materials," I said.

"For what they're paying you to do it and be photographed coming in and going out plus talk about how wonderful it was in the next five interviews, I might as well be. I'm not kidding—you could live for a few years on what they forked over," he said. "You wouldn't have to do another film for a long time."

"Yeah," I said as the doorbell rang, "but I *like* doing films."

Still, it was intriguing. So I went.

From the second the driver they sent for me pulled up to the building, it was like going into a science laboratory. I thought maybe it'd be more like going to the spa for a haircut or something, but that was not it at all.

They strapped me into a chair in nothing but a robe. The electrodes were attached all over my body. I told myself to remember this scenario for a future film—the power play aspects could be very hot.

"How many people have been through the treatment so far?" I asked.

"A few," the young woman attaching leads to my chest said. "Normally, we'd need to shave you, but…" she says. Her hand lingered a bit too long on my stomach, which I took as a compliment.

When the doctor came in, I thought he'd be attractive or at least powerful and handsome—a part of me was still thinking that this would be some kind of spa experience. Instead he was old and kind of hunched over and had glasses. His voice, though, was remarkable. I thought to myself that I would love to hear him narrate a book broadcast.

"Are you comfortable?" he asked. I tried to place the accent. Austrian (well, back when Austria existed, I mean)? Like that ancient movie star in all the action films.

"Yes," I said. I thought, again, about how hot this whole thing was—being restrained. He could do anything to me he wanted right now with his super science. When my body started to respond to that, I had to cool things down a bit. I used the old math trick.

"Good," he said. "Then let's begin."

From behind me I heard a hissing sound and then there was a soreness as the base of my neck. I started to say "ow" but almost instantly my vision began to blur and my shoulders went slack.

The next thing I knew, I was waking up. I felt more relaxed than I had in a very long time. Even my fingers felt a little rubbery and loose.

Two young women were removing my restraints.

"How do you feel?" a tall woman in a white coat asked me.

"I feel fantastic," I said.

"Good; we do so aim to please," she said. "Ladies, if you'll…"

The young women walked me to a small room where my clothes were. As I changed into them, I couldn't remember the last time I'd ever felt so relaxed, so thoroughly rested.

On the way out, they gave me a gift bag with a gorgeous antique-style watch in it. "Your gift from us. And it tracks your walking step count and overall circulatory health!" the young woman at the reception desk said. It was like a fantastic spa.

Everyone I met for the next month said how rested I looked.

# OLVER

I awake from a dream that someone is choking me.

I know, as we all do, that the dream likely only lasted a few min-utes, but it seems as if all night someone has had their hand around my throat. I sit up, the cover falling away from my chest. I reach out next to me, already knowing that Olver isn't there. My hand rests on the cover, still undisturbed.

I get up and pad to the small table near the wall for water, the cold air prickling my naked chest. I grew up in houses where there was al-ways a table right next to either side of the bed. I had always set things up this way in my own homes. Here, though, you aren't expected to get anything for yourself. Everything comes with a snap of the finger, or the ring of a bell. That means that nothing is close to the bed. There are tables next to the chairs scattered about the place, but they always have huge sprays of flowers on them, meant for decoration, not work.

I find a chair and sit, holding the glass of water close to my chest even though its chill stings my skin. Again, I notice how cold the air is. It begins to register that it is far too cold to be comfortable. I see my breath frost the glass. I pull my legs up into the chair and rest my head on my knees, something I haven't done since I was a child. I could easily get up and get a shirt, or a sweater; I could even ring for a servant to come and bring me one from across the room.

Instead I hold the water with one hand, and with the other I keep sliding my fingers over my neck, amazed that I don't find welts. I can still feel the hand of another.

The floor rumbles a bit, and I feel warm air rise in plumes all around me.

"There you are, beloved," Olver says as he enters the room. I never bothered to turn on any lights, but I can see from his outline that he has a suit on. He comes across to me.

"It's cold," is all I can think to say.

He kneels down in front of me and rubs his hands on my thighs.

"A small problem with the heating. I was summoned to come help the engineers deal with it. It is okay now. Come back to bed," he says. He stands and extends his hand to me. I set the glass on the edge of the small table near the chair, knowing that when I wake, it won't be there anymore. Someone will come in the night and whisk it away. I take Olver's hand and let him lead me back to bed.

He toes out of his shoes, slides the jacket off, and pulls back the cover for me to slide in. Already the room is warm enough that my shoulders relax and my knees don't creak. He tucks the cover around me, then lays himself down next to me. He kisses my forehead in a way that I find comforting, and pushes the hair back from my face.

Even as I drift off, I still feel someone's hand around my throat.

# LIKE SOMETHING FROM A DREAM

Do you believe that there are some people who should be punished for disobeying their government? The man asks me.

I do.

Do you believe that there are people who should be put to death for disobeying their government? The man asks me.

I do.

Are you now or have you ever been a member of the military? The man asks.

I haven't.

Are you now or have you ever been a member of an organization that had the goal of overthrowing the government?

I haven't.

Are you now or have you ever been a communist?

I haven't.

Are you now or have you ever been a socialist?

I haven't.

Are you now or have you ever been an anarchist?

I haven't.

Are you a homosexual?

I am not.

Are you married?

I'm not.

Do you have any children?

I don't.

The man stands and extends his hand to me.

Welcome aboard.

This is day 1

# THE PAST

Old science fiction movies always predict a future where people don't have sex drives. Or, if they do, the most they get up to is vanilla, straight, missionary sex with the covers slightly askew so a bit of ass cheek shows.

I wonder what some of those people who were making science fiction back in the early 21st century would think to know what the world we live in today is actually like.

I did my first OTK spank video when I was 15. For those of you who are out of the loop on that kind of thing, that's a video where an older, larger man takes a smaller subservient person (in my case, a barely-legal by updated consent laws for purposes of working, nearly-skeletally-skinny male) over their knee and spanks them using their hand or other object. Sometimes they have narratives ("I told you to be in by curfew") and sometimes not.

This is a thing people like to watch to get it up.

A thing they secretly think about.

That day, the man playing my father for purposes of the video beat me with his hand, and then with a belt, and then with a heavy leather strap with metal studs on it, until my ass was so raw and red that the director stopped the shoot even though the script called for one last instrument, a thin wooden cane, to be used for another five minutes.

This was not even the most unusual thing I did sexually that week.

All of this while around me shuttles ran regularly from New York taking families on sightseeing day-trips to the moon. While the first commercial flight to the moons of Jupiter was just about to dock.

It makes me look back at some of those old movies and wonder what the characters were doing off screen. What the space princess asked the smuggling scoundrel to do to her. What kinds of things the slutty space captain really got up to with his green alien women in his quarters.

In all of my years, here's what I've discovered: there is no such thing as a person who is actually so virtuous that they don't have at least one thing they like sexually that would shock the hell out of their best friends. I watch those old space operas and I wonder why they only ever seem to kiss and hug given how often they face certain death.

I bet the one with the pointy ears secretly likes to be choked until he finishes.

Don't even get me started on the vigilante superheroes.

# SYLAS

Today, I am taken to another area that is under construction. Sylas sits among the unshielded cables and wiring, the unfinished deck plating.

"Why here?" I ask.

Sylas shrugs, "it was the closest unfinished segment from where I had a meeting this morning."

"Oh?" I ask and sit down next to him.

"Yes," he says and sighs.

I sense something is wrong. "What was this meeting about?" I ask.

"You."

"What about me?" I ask.

"There are some in the organization that believe my attempt to contact you, that bringing you to our cause, is a mistake," he says without looking at me.

"And what do you believe?" I ask.

Silence settles over us.

"I think that—," he begins to say. Just then, though there are two sharp clangs of steel on steel. He stands. Then there is another clang. Without saying anything he grabs my wrist and we are both running.

"What's going on?" I ask. He shushes me without stopping.

I have to run at full speed to keep up with him. We turn corners and slide through tiny crevices between unfinished walls. Eventually we make it to a room where the walls haven't been put in. The huge trunks of cables all run into this room, and the wiring forms the web of some huge spider along the ceiling and the floor. He stops but doesn't let go.

"What is—?" I start to ask but he shushes me again. I start to protest, but he's closed his eyes and is listening.

After what seems like days, he opens his eyes again.

"They have found us," he whispers.

"Who?" I ask.

"Single chime—that can only mean someone high up. Someone with technology."

"It couldn't just have been a worker?"

"We control all the workers," Sylas says.

"All of them?" I ask. He nods.

"With technology, what does that mean?"

"They were tracking one of us," he says. "I suspect you."

It's only then that I notice he's pulled a knife from one of his pockets.

"Whoa," I say and back up.

"Before I walk out onto any street, I check and double check that I am not wearing a tracking device. Strip," he commands.

"Wait, I'm not going to—," I start to protest.

"Strip. Now. Or…" he trails off and looks at the knife. Every bit of closeness and connection I've ever felt from him gone in an instant.

As I do, he takes the knife and raps the blade on the wall twice.

I stand there naked. I notice that Sylas is looking everywhere but at me. I know he would prefer me to be somehow embarrassed, to try to cover my body. This isn't even the first time I've been naked in the middle of a construction area because someone was worried I was wearing a recording device, let alone anything else. He picks up my clothes and passes them out into what looks like an empty corridor. Hands take them from around the corner. Sylas has already taken off his jacket and he hands it to me. I sit down and drape it across my lap.

"This will only take a second," Sylas says.

The clothes come back around the corner. Sylas leans out and he's nodding at whatever is being said to him. He hands my clothes back to me.

"We have to go. Now," he says.

"What happened?"

"Get dressed!" he whispers through clenched teeth. "Not only did they track you, they've sent a squad. They must know." I notice that my shirt is now missing its third button.

The instant I have my second shoe on, he pulls me down another corridor. We're around several more corners, and moving through empty spaces that will be walls eventually. I notice it's getting colder as we run. It might be my imagination, but I swear I can hear the heavy thudding of boots in the distance.

Eventually we reach a section that is mostly complete. It sticks out after being in so many unfinished superstructure areas. Sylas taps in a code very quickly and a door as large as a wall opens. Just past the door a yawning cavernous space opens up, and in it are a few of the smaller submersible craft I've seen people use for construction on the station's outside.

Sylas drags me to one and fumbles with the keypad for a moment. "Come on, come on, come on,"

The hatch lifts up and Sylas jumps into the pilot's seat. He pulls me down into the cockpit with the hatch closing just above my face. The hatch barely has time to click into place before the outer door opens wide and water starts to spill in.

As the little sub starts to jostle about, slowly coming up off the floor of the bay, I can see shadows at the window to the main door leading in. At this rate, they'll have to completely push the water out to get in, then get any sub they want to use to chase after us up and running, then flood the lock again. That'll give us a good head start.

I cover my face with my hands.

Before the sub is completely under the water, Sylas is already maneuvering it toward the outer door. We move very quickly out and away from the station. He's already got the tiny thing up to full speed before we're safe distance away from the station's exterior.

"Hopefully there aren't any patrols near…" Sylas starts to say as the water near us ripples. I see the tail end of some kind of torpedo go by.

"They're shooting at us?" I ask.

"This is a good thing in some ways," Sylas says, sending the tiny sub into a series of maneuvers that make me sick to my stomach. "If they're firing, they don't think anyone important is on board. That means that they might not know that they were tracking you specifically."

"Or that they just don't care," I say.

"That is a distinct possibility," Sylas says. He's slamming the little submarine through moves that would break a larger submarine in half.

Sylas keeps dodging in toward the skin of the station, trying to make our pursuers run into an antenna or a large outcrop.

I do hear a large rumble behind us at one point. But then there are more torpedoes. More dodging. More maneuvers. This goes on for hours it feels like.

"The current," Sylas says.

"What?" I ask as he slams the controls forward and the little submarine dives steeply.

"The deep current. IF we can get into it, we'll lose them."

"Why is that?"

"Because they know that nothing they have is in any way capable of withstanding the force of the deep current's speed and strength."

"Can this?" I ask, thumping the door.

Sylas doesn't answer.

As if it will help, I grip the nearby panic handle tighter.

The dive continues and continues until eventually we are slammed sideways and then spun around. When the lights come back up, Sylas has dialed the engines way back but I can tell we're still moving very fast.

"There," he says. "Welcome to The River, the fastest current we have ever clocked on the planet. Let's just hope—," the little craft shudders. There is the moan of the metal being compressed. One of the gauges shatters. The tiny ship bucks like a horse a few times. "They'd be crazy to follow us in here."

"Doesn't that mean we're crazy for being here?" I ask.

Sylas smiles. "I've run this current before. Eventually it leads to a set of trenches where we can lay low for a bit until my people can get to us."

"And what then?" I ask.

Sylas purses his lips. "Perhaps we are lucky. That they knew they were tracking someone very important but maybe that tracking signal wasn't specific. Perhaps Olver doesn't know yet that you are...sympathetic to my cause."

I can't help but hear the doubt in his voice.

The submarine bucked wildly for another ten minutes until we exited the jet current. Once outside I relax. My hands had turned white. I flex my fingers to try to get some blood back into them and flick a few switches to get a view behind us.

"They have given up pursuit," Sylas says. "At least for now."

"What do we do?" I ask, trying to get control of my breathing.

"That is a very good question," he says. "I think perhaps we should take refuge on the sea floor for a bit."

"Can this little thing go that deep?" I ask.

"No," he says. "That is what we should do, but circumstances prevent that from being a viable alternative. Therefore," he says, flicks a few switches, and the lights go out around us.

"What are you doing?!"

"The next best thing to hiding in a cave...turning off anything that would allow them to find us using satellites," Sylas says. "It shouldn't take more than say thirty minutes for them to give up on us. In that time, we shouldn't drift more than a few hundred feet down. We're nowhere near our crush depth, so we should be safe for the time being. The only real problem we have is the cold," he says, reaching behind us into a small compartment and pulling out two blankets. He hands one to me saying, "and if a large animal should consider taking a bite of us."

I start scanning the ocean around us intently. He laughs. "What?" I ask.

"The chances of something large enough to consider us a safe bet for dinner being up at this depth are very slim." He snuggles down into his blanket. Outside the window, just at the edge of my vision, something bulky swims past us. Despite what he has said, I cannot stop scanning the water. I look over and see that his eyes are closed.

"What if they don't give up?" I ask.

"The heat we are giving off right now is so little that they would likely misread us as a turtle or something unless they were close enough to see us with a naked eye. And if the universe has conspired to make that happen, for them to be that close, then I think we can infer that our entire enterprise is doomed," he says without opening his eyes. "You should try to get some rest."

My body is still coursing with adrenaline. I can feel my heart, still. "How can you possibly be able to rest right now? I'm filled with adrenaline."

He turns slightly in his seat so that we can see one another. Without opening his eyes, he asks, "the first time you had to...perform... were you not nervous?"

"I was geeked out of my mind. I barely remember it," I say.

He nods. "How did you get through that moment?"

"During the training, they told me that it would probably be like that, so they told me to...oh, I see," I said. They'd told me to try to ride on top of the energy like a wave—to not get caught up in it, but to skim along the surface of it. To use it. I started doing the breathing exercises they'd taught me so long ago.

"That's better," he says.

Slowly, the shaking stops, and it gets more and more difficult to hear my heart. He hasn't said anything in a while and I think he's asleep but as soon as I stop the breathing exercises and switch back over to just regular breathing, he says, "good."

Outside the bubble, always just at the edge of my vision, things swim by. I can never make out what they are, but just from the impression of their sizes I can tell that we must be near some major route that lots of animals use. Like a highway. I'm sure someone with a degree in whatever would be able to dig up the right word, but for me, this is a new idea.

"So you never did answer the question," I say.

"Which question is that?"

"Whether or not *you* think it's a mistake to have brought me in," I say.

Sylas thinks for a moment. "Ultimately, the problem is what we do after we have control."

"What do you mean?" I ask.

"Before it was decided that I would, you had asked me if I would be President after we take power," Sylas says. "I said no, and you asked me why. Getting people to agree that there must be change is never hard. No matter how good things are for anyone, they will always feel things could be better," he says. "So all someone who has a vision ever truly has to do is start a conversation and press a point about something universal. 'Don't you feel that taxes are too high?' or 'wouldn't you like it if more people felt the way you do about' and then insert whatever the latest social issue is. It isn't difficult to gain followers," Sylas says. I thought about all the times I'd seen politicians say those exact same things. "The problem is what do you do once the revolution is over. The type of personality that will say 'there must be change' is not the type of personality that is cut out for establishing rule. They tend to be at odds with one another."

"So what are you going to do?" I ask. Without realizing it, I'd snuggled down into my blanket and turned myself to face him. On some level, from an outside point of view, we must look like boys at their first sleepover, chatting into the night.

"What any sane person would do—I've set up two different teams. I think this is where many of the revolutions have failed in the past—the incoming power group tried to then become the ruling group."

"Do the groups know about one another?" I ask.

"Yes," he says, "but they don't like one another very much. I fear for what may happen once it becomes time for the hand off."

The cabin is quiet for a bit.

"What will happen to me?" I ask. "Which group am I in?"

"That entirely depends upon you," Sylas says. I notice it didn't take him long to answer—he's thought about this, already.

"What if I want to leave?"

"Nothing will stop you if that is your choice," he says. "You have my word on that." It's hard not to hear the disappointment in his voice. "Do you love him?"

"Who, Olver?" I ask. He nods. "You're asking the wrong person. I don't know that I know what love even is."

"Do you care about what happens to him?" Sylas asks.

"I...some part of me does," I say.

"Then why do you help us?"

"I don't know," I say, and turn over to face away from him. "I'm not some..."

"Some what?" he asks.

"I don't know," I say.

"No, you do. What were you about to say?"

"I. Don't. Know," I say, turning to face him.

After a while he exhales loudly. "Terrorist?" he asks.

I don't say anything.

"It seems to me that word all depends on what side one is on," he says.

We both listen to the sounds of the water all around us.

"Revolution always comes from strange places. Places you wouldn't expect," he says. "I read that, back on Earth, centuries ago, there was a man who became one of the most successful leaders of a group that people called terrorists. Before he had been swept up into the movement, though, he was a novelist."

"Was he any good?" I ask.

Sylas laughs. "He certainly was at being a revolutionary...the novels, not so much," he says with a grin. I laugh.

"Are you…attracted to him?"

"Why do you want to know?" I ask.

"Because I am curious about a man like you. What drives you."

"I'm just like anyone else," I say.

"Are you?"

"I am attracted to him. His mind. His power."

"His body?"

"After this long doing what I do…after the life I've lived," I say, "you start to see that a body is not something attractive or not. It simply is."

Something beeps. With the whole sub powered down, it startles me. Sylas pulls a square block of metal from a tiny cupboard behind my head. He flicks a switch.

"Go," he says.

"Squid running. We have lock 86. Hurry," the voice says.

"What—," I start to ask.

"Satellite communicator. We've managed to get control of one of the older telcom units. My men have control of one of the airlocks for a time. We will have to sprint to get there and get back into the station." He starts flipping switches and the sub comes back to life.

"But what if we're still being tracked?"

"My men are creating a diversion as we speak. One of our subs will lead them a merry chase and then lay low for a few days until they move on to something else," Sylas says. He jerks the wheel around and guns the engine. The sudden acceleration makes me go giddy and I smile despite the danger.

Sylas does as well.

"But won't they be in just as much danger of dying as we are?" I ask.

"Unlike us, that sub is always packed for just such an event. It has food and heaters that don't run from the submarine's power supply. For them this will be the equivalent of a nice camping trip. Provided they aren't sunk before making the ridges."

Sylas slings us through maneuver after maneuver, eventually bringing us in to a tiny docking bay at the very base of the station itself. I try not to think about how far down we are.

Once inside, his men rush us up through corridors and hatchways and eventually we wind up coming out of a hatch into an alleyway behind a busy street and to a house that I recognize.

●

After a hot shower, Sylas, Falma, Salil and I are sat around a table eating a hot meal that she made. I don't know if it's the adrenaline or the cook, herself, but I've never tasted any food as good as this is.

A man enters without knocking and leans down to whisper something in Sylas's ear. Sylas's face goes blank for a moment, then I watch him try to get control of his emotions. "Something has come up," he says as he stands. "If you'll excuse me for a moment." He leaves with the messenger.

Salil is unconcerned. He is making one of his celery spears dance along the edge of the plate as though nothing in the room has changed. I hear him humming something under his breath.

"What's that?" I ask.

He looks at me, surprised to be addressed.

"The song you were humming, what is it?"

"Oh," he says, relieved. "'The Blue Danube.' Do you know it?"

I hum the bit that I know. His face breaks into a smile that would light a darkened hallway. "Yes! Yes, that's the tune." He bites into the celery spear. "It's my favorite. Did you know that tempo, the three beats, is called a Waltz? I love it. It's my favorite tempo to dance to."

"You like to dance?" I ask.

He looks at me as if the most obvious thing in the world has just been said. "It is my whole reason for existing. I love to dance." He stands and moves to the open area between the door and the table, then begins to sway and step as he sings "The Blue Danube'" He dances as if no one else is in the room, losing himself completely in the accenting of a beat here, a note there. I've been with dancers. Lots of them. I've seen this level of selflessness only a few times before, though. He isn't the best dancer I've ever seen, but he is earnest in his love of the movement. With training, he could be one of the best.

"Do you like to dance?" he asks. He pauses and cocks his head.

"I used to," I say. "I haven't in a long time."

"Why not?" he says, stretching.

"I don't know, to be honest. I guess I just haven't wanted to."

He puts his hands on his tiny, narrow hips. "That's no reason not to do something." He extends his hands out toward me. "Come, dance."

"No, that's alright," I say.

He walks over and takes my hand, pulling me up. "No. No sitting this one out. You will dance."

"But I'm out of practice," I say.

He pulls me to standing and then moves so that we are together. He begins to sing the same waltz again and then move us both. I don't know how long we're dancing like that, but when Sylas returns I'm smiling. Sylas laughs and claps. "I see it didn't take long for him to convince you to dance."

Salil smiles, too, as we separate. "He's out of practice," the boy says.

"I would imagine. The trip out here to be with us alone took a long time," Sylas says. We all sit back down to the table. "Were you a dancer?" Sylas asks me.

"No," I say. "Never."

"It is his passion," Sylas says, putting his hand on Salil's shoulder and shaking him a bit. "Go, now, and let us talk," he says. Salil stands once more and leaves. Staring after him, Sylas says, "what a world it would be if we could all simply devote ourselves to an art form."

"He's very earnest," I say. "With training, he could be quite good."

"This is my hope. I want to make him happy. Simply by existing, he proved to us that there is a way forward and we of the movement owe him for that. Our debt is to make him comfortable and happy the rest of his days."

"What happened?" I ask.

Sylas's face darkens and he turns to me. "One of the independent cells from the lowest decks was uncovered. A member thought he could trust someone who turned out to be an informer."

I panic. "We should get out of here! They'll be…"

Sylas puts his hand on my shoulder. "Relax. They had time to follow protocol and were all dead before the soldiers gained access. This was not a main cell. While I hate that they lost their lives, they were not affiliated closely enough to give up any information even if they had survived. We are safe."

I try to relax back into my cushion. Sylas takes a small date cake and sips some tea, but then sees that I am not relaxed. "Still, we should get you back soon just in case Olver decides to leave the palace. Come, I'll take you home."

●

"What has he told you?" Sylas asks.

Days later, we're sitting in one of the café back rooms that he assures me are completely safe as the whole block is controlled by his people. I can't stop looking at the door expecting that at any minute Olver's men will come through and then we'll all be executed.

"He said that Earth forces arrived in orbit and then destroyed everything. That he was the only one from his family who made it out alive."

Sylas sips his tea. "And what do you think?"

"I'm not sure what you're asking," I say.

"Of that story," Sylas asks. "It doesn't strike you as a bit odd?"

"In what way?" I ask.

"This planet is 98 and some odd percent water."

"So?"

"So what could this planet possibly have, besides water, that the Earth forces would want?" Sylas asks.

It's such a simple question, and yet it hits me hard.

"Why would Earth send out an attack force to the absolute edge of the known worlds, as it is now, but especially as it was then, just to fight some jumped up revolutionary of a planet that is mostly just water?"

"I...I don't know," I say.

Sylas leans back in his chair and sighs.

"What do you know?" I ask.

"Why did you come here?" Sylas asks.

"Olver asked me to."

"Be honest," Sylas says.

"I am."

"*Why* did you come here?"

The silence stretches out between us.

"Where would the son of a dead, rebellious overseer of a station at the absolute edge of the map come up with the kind of money that attracted you, someone who was used to such things as money and attention, to come and be with him?" Sylas asks.

I felt stupid. I said nothing.

After a long while, Sylas tilted his head to the side and said, "It's a mineral that we have here. Or, I should say, an amalgamation of several minerals that tend to clump together into one conglomeration. A highly efficient and compact fuel source that allows the faster than light drives to work without being fifty times the size they are. Because of the unique properties of the pressure and water contents on the cooling of the molten rock that comes up from the core, it is found on very few planets," Sylas says. "And never in the abundance that it is found here." He sips his tea. "If you go back and look at the long history of Earth, conflict almost always arises for this very reason. A region has a resource that another region lacks. The second region builds a force, be it by land or air or sea, to go and, by force, procure that resource."

"But why did they destroy Olver's family?"

"His father had the nerve to say to the Earth, pay more for the resource or I will not only stop shipping it to you, I will start producing it for myself and selling it to others for my own benefit," Sylas says.

"But...if that were the case, after they destroyed him, why didn't they take over the station?"

"Now you begin to see. Go further," Sylas says.

"I don't understand."

"In our grand leader Olver's origin story, there is a vast Earth fleet that arrives and bombs the little surface that this world had, destroying his family and their grand palace," Sylas says.

"Yes," I say.

"Considering what I've told you about the fuel, does anything about that story sound odd to you?"

It takes me a moment, and I'm embarrassed. "How did they do that without igniting the fuel?" I ask.

Sylas nods and I recognize that there is a place deep inside me that craves his approval. "Precisely. What if I told you that they never intended the devastation to be as large as it was?"

"An accident?"

Sylas nods again.

"What would make the forces that wiped the last bit of land off the surface of this world suddenly stop their massacre?" Sylas asks. "Why has there been peace this long time unless the marauding force was getting what they wanted? This colony is, after all, still an Earth colony, is it not?"

It took me a moment, I'm not proud to say. But then it dawned on me. "It was just supposed to be an intimidation, wasn't it?" I ask.

Sylas nods again, this time smiling. "In order to save face, they had to pretend that the mass destruction had been their intent all along. Needless to say, though, they were highly motivated to find a quick, peaceful end to the hostilities."

I see it. "Olver is working with the Earth. He's giving them what they want."

Sylas smiled and I wish I could say that I was immune to such things, but his approval made me feel warm. "A puppet king intimidated onto a throne bought by his own family's blood completely by accident," Sylas says. "I'm sure he spins you tales of his bravery in defending this planet, our young lion, but the truth is he surrendered the second he could make clear contact through the jammed frequencies. In return, the Earth forces halted their attack and he was quickly installed as the ruler of this little world. So long as the shipments are made on time, no one cares what he does here."

"So when people disappear…" I start.

"So long as the shipments are made on time…" Sylas repeats.

I can't find anything to say. The enormity of what's going on hits me.

"What is even more interesting," Sylas continues though I'm still dizzy, "is that he has actually upped the quota, ships the same amount back to Earth, and sells the excess to certain…unsavory…groups. The amount of wealth flowing into his coffers is staggering. The palace is opulent, yes, but the people still starve in the streets. Where, one must wonder, is the balance of all that vast wealth going?"

My mind instantly flashed to the hangar with all the new mechs sitting side by side, silent, waiting.

"I think I know," I say.

"Go on," Sylas says. I get the feeling he already knows, but I want to show him that I know, too.

"The mechs. Rows and rows of them. Brand new machines equipped with these telepathic interface things I've never even heard of."

Sylas smiles and nods then finishes his tea.

"What's he going to do with them?" I ask.

"Hopefully, nothing," Sylas says as he stands, "because we will stop him before he can, saving us all from the same fate as those who foolishly followed his father into the very rebellion that installed Olver on his throne in the first place." He turns on his heel and I grab my coat and follow him out.

# THE PAST

There was a fire. I don't think about it often, but when I do it takes a few days to get back to even, if you know what I mean. And usually some fairly strong pharmaceuticals.

We had just finished a particularly long shoot. We'd gone through three different guys who swore up and down that they would be good on camera—that they could get it up and get off on cue.

Normally, that wouldn't even be a problem. There are all kinds of pills and gels for that kind of thing. This was a super low budget production, though. We didn't have that kind of money. Not to mention, too, that these guys had sworn up and down that they were good to go.

Now, of course, I work with directors and crews that know to bring all of that kind of stuff anyway. This was a different time, though.

Once we finally got a guy who could finish on cue and got finished, we were all exhausted. The director also owned the house, so he just told everyone that they could crash for the night and get on the road in the morning. He told me that I could sleep in the big bed with him if I wanted. I was so tired I didn't even mind that he wanted to blow me before we slept.

What we didn't count on was the subpar wiring in the house. The crew who stayed left a lot of stuff plugged in to charge. What we didn't know was that the regular load of the appliances of this very very old house were already taxing the interior grid to the maximum. The overload was just too much for few faults that were in the place.

The fire started somewhere near the living room, where we'd been doing the bulk of the filming, they told us all later. Those of us that lived, any way.

By the time I woke up, I was half on fire myself.

The few of us who made it out got far enough away and called the emergency in, but it was too late. The house was never meant to have lasted as long as it did. It went up quickly.

In the hospital, once they got my pain managed, they let me know about the extent of the burns.

Facial reconstruction would be necessary.

At this point, of course, the technology existed to do this kind of thing in a day or so. Rather than see it as a terrible thing, though, I saw it as an opportunity. So, rather than just let any old shmuck have at me, I used a lot of the money I'd squirreled away and got a specialist. We went through noses and cheekbones like it was a menu. When he turned the screen around to face me the last time, I saw it—there was the face I'd always wanted.

At the same time, I contacted the guy who'd been handling my bookings. I told him to start making some noise about my new face. Rather than try to hide it, I would make it the centerpiece of a re-emergence.

They finished the face and by the end of that week, just a week after the fire, I looked at the face I'd always wanted to have.

It turned out to be massively popular, as well. My bookings went through the roof. People loved looking at what appeared to be an upper-class guy just barely old enough to be away at college who could do the things I'd learned to do over time.

I started having more surgeries. We changed the way my chest looked. We changed the thickness of my ankles so that they looked prettier in the shot. We changed the prominence of my hip bones so that I looked more muscular through the waist. The money left as soon as it came in, but time after time I looked in the mirror and found the person I felt I was in my head staring back at me.

Eventually, we were done. That's when my fees went astronomical. People wanted me to do all kinds of things. Even though I didn't have to, I said yes to so many of them. Almost all, really.

I had made myself.

I wanted everyone to have the pleasure of seeing.

# OLVER

Waking to find Olver no longer in bed has become so routine that I don't even feel for him, anymore. I stand, put on my robe and slippers and walk down the long hallway to the table beside the window. I sit without saying anything and put my hand over the top of his.

"Bad?" I ask.

The dim light coming in from the barrier lights casts deep shadows across his face, but I can still see his eyes. He nods. His servants already know that this is where he'll wind up, and so there are two glasses and a pitcher of cold water on the table. I pour one for him and one for me. The water is chilled to the point of hurting as it goes down, a sensation I've come to relish.

"I suppose that, in many ways," Olver is saying, "I was lucky. The Earthers, thrice damn their name, in destroying my father and all of the men who were in control during that time, they cleared the way for my own rule." He sits down. One of my favorite things during these late night talks is seeing the light reflect on his face from the window. His extraordinarily handsome brow. "That doesn't mean that I haven't had to fight every inch along the way. There have been wars to fight at the conference tables all along."

"But you've won," I say.

He pours more water into my glass, then sips from his own. "I know it must seem that way, but at every turn there have been compromises.

Things I had to give up in order to accomplish the things that need to be done. And the tiny aggressions of maneuvering. Sometimes it's as if they don't understand," he says, gesturing all around us with his glass, "that we're talking about real people, not simply things to be manipulated and moved at will."

"There are factions?" I ask.

"Oh, yes," he says, laughing bitterly. "Every decision I make is watched carefully and confirms *someone's* darkest suspicion. In their own lives, they want to be understood, seen in the best possible light, but when it comes to me, so many of them see only some powermad dilettante...or worse, an uncaring idiot...a...what was that old expression? A bull in a china shop?" He sipped more water as if trying to get the taste of those words from his mouth. Then he sets the glass down and puts his hand on top of mine. "This is why I am so glad you are here. I so badly need someone in my life that I can talk with who is away from all of the petty intrigues."

My thoughts immediately go to Sylas. Olver leans forward and brings my hand to his lips. He stands and gently pulls me to my feet, then into his arms. I embrace him in return, thinking of the things that Sylas had said about him. But then his lips find my neck, then my collar bone and all of my thoughts go away.

"This will be fun," Olver's voice says in my earpiece. There is still a bit of stiffness along my jaw where the tiny plate of metal that takes the vibration of my voice back through the wires to him rests and Doctor Farook Hamza, the head of medical issues for all of Olver's pilots, a kind man with glasses and enormous hands watches my vital information on their screens in a control room across the hangar bay.

"So you say." I'm nervous. The cockpit of the mech hasn't yet filled with the oxygen saturated liquid that will also form the connection between my body's motions and the robots movements, but I know it's coming. I can't relax.

"As I told you, this is the newer system. Whereas the connection device that I put on your head in my older mech provided at best 75% connection between my thoughts and the motions of the robot, this system provides for 100%, making the mech faster, more agile. Your own reflexes will become the reflexes of the mech, beloved." The liquid is up to my waist. I'm starting to panic. "The system my mech functioned with could never fully connect with its pilot's central nervous system. I had to use controls, as you saw, to make it move at any given time. With this system, the sensors along the robot's skin become the thermoreceptors, the mechanoreceptors, all of the functions that your own skin has, transferring their information to your cortex to be processed. These new mechs become the body of the pilot. Man and machine are one thing."

My breathing rate is up. My heart pounds against my ribs as if it wants out. The liquid is up to my chest.

"Try to remember that your body existed in a very similar environment for the first nine months of its existence. While there might be a moment of panic, it will remember very quickly and adapt."

There is a quiet hissing behind my head somewhere and then the chamber begins to fill. "Your instinct will be to hold your breath," Olver says in my ear. "This will go much easier, though, if, instead, you simply take one big inhale as soon as the liquid reaches just above your nose. I know you've had to make yourself do it these first few times, but eventually it'll become second nature."

It's up to my chest now, and still, no matter how many times, surprisingly warm. When I had envisioned this, though, I had pictured the liquid being cold. In my ear, I hear Olver's small laugh, the one he does when we're alone in bed together. It helps. The liquid is up to my chin, now. Then above my lips. I'm having to fight the urge in my legs and arms to flee. My eyes lock on the handle to the front of the compartment that would open the cockpit and let me out. The liquid covers the tip of my nose. "Just a second more, my love," Olver says. "And…now." Somehow he knows exactly when my entire nose is under the liquid. I try to force myself to open my mouth, to inhale the liquid, but my body will not listen. Instead it bucks wildly against the harness. I try again, but my mouth won't open. Instead, my arms flail a bit. "Stop fighting it, my love," Olver whispers in my ear. "Trust in me," he says.

Somehow I manage to get my mouth to open and to inhale. A microsecond of utter blinding panic sets in as my body is convinced it is drowning. But then I feel my lungs fill with oxygen. I close my mouth and breathe the liquid down through my nose. Again, a fleeting sense of panic, but again my lungs fill. In fact, I don't recall ever feeling them this full and energized ever before. I feel like I could run a marathon. "There you are, beloved," Olver says. "Excellent. Doctor Hamza tells me that he has rarely seen a neurophysiological connection this strong. You are synchronizing very well." Hearing him say such things makes me proud of myself. "Continue to breathe while the systems finish their connections." My muscles feel tight, compact, coiled and ready to spring into action. Slowly, I begin to see the suggestions of terrain in front of me, in my peripheral, and below me. The liquid fades away and I start to see the hangar around me as if the mech were no longer there. It makes me dizzy at first.

"The sensors are beginning their handshake with your own optic nerves, now. You should be able to see as though the mecha's body was your own. Is that happening?" Olver asks. It's more than just happening; I can see in sharp definition no matter what direction I turn my head. It is as if I'm floating above the deck with nothing around me. "Be very careful during this initial phase, my love," Olver says. "You are now connected to the machine. Your slightest muscle twitch will be translated to the limbs of the mech."

I feel it. I am fifteen feet tall. The hangar, which normally towers above me, is now almost not big enough to contain me. I want to sprint, I want to jump. I have never felt this powerful in my entire life. I reach out, extending my hand so I can look at the palm. The mech's huge hand comes into view. Through it, I can tell that it is cold outside. A part of my brain tells me the exact temperature, but what makes me laugh incredulously is that it isn't just raw data on a screen—I am experiencing the coldness of the air around the machine.

"Doctor Hamza says you are reaching the upper limit of what any of our pilots have achieved in terms of synchronization. Careful, my love, or he'll recruit you away from me," Olver says. The pride in his voice makes me want to stand taller, to somehow make the machine synchronize with me to the fullest.

Over the next half hour, Olver and Doctor Hamza run me through a series of tests to determine if I'm synchronized well. Move this hand, raise this foot, rotate this wrist so many degrees, etc. At every turn, Olver says the doctor is telling him that I am some kind of natural at this, a mecha savant. When Olver tells me to power down the armor and the liquid begins to drain, I feel disappointed. I have to stop myself from protesting, from asking for a few more minutes as if it were some thrill ride and I a child to be indulged. The sensation of power that the mecha instilled in me was intoxicating. I wanted to run with it, to leap over things, to smash barriers.

"All in good time, beloved," Olver says. I have to make myself gag out the last of the oxygenated liquid onto the deck as soon as the cock-pit hatch opens. "I apologize," Olver says, handing me a towel. I catch the look of incredulousness from one of the nearby techs to see the leader performing so menial a task. I step out onto the platform, having to use all my will to not collapse as my mind adjusts to being so tiny, so fragile once more. I nearly tumble over the side, though; I overstep, still feeling some of the power of the mech's legs in my own feeble muscles. Olver catches me and laughs. He takes the towel back and begins to dry my hair while pulling me in close to him. A small part of me protests the treatment—I am not a child. Another part of me, though, is deeply fulfilled by it.

"An excellent ride," Olver says.

"Was it?" I ask. For a second, I'm surprised at how much I want him to be proud of me.

"Yes, my love," he says, pulling me in even closer. His eyes meet mine and then he is kissing me.

"What has you so upset?" I ask Olver as he finishes dressing. I watch him from the bed. Watching a man dress is one of my favorite things, second only to watching them undress, and Olver does not disappoint. From how he handles a shoe before putting it on to the way that he smooths his shirt down once it is over his shoulders, he does everything in exactly the right order, with just a bit of personality. Not so much as to make him seem odd, but enough that I can see his depth. I imagine him even as a young boy being dressed by others but secretly developing little rituals of his own on the days when he was allowed to do it by himself.

"Nothing, my beloved." He ties his tie. I can see him repeating something to himself under his breath. I know that, were he in his own rooms, someone would be doing these things for him.

His shoulders are high, though. I know that if I touched them, they would be tight. I can see the worry in his eyes.

"Tell me," I say.

"Truly," he says without looking back at me. "It is nothing."

"Please?" I ask, standing and putting myself directly in his line of sight in the mirror.

He looks at my reflection. "There is a trial today. A man may be sentenced to be executed. I don't want you around that sort of thing," he says.

"What has this man done?" I ask.

"That isn't something we should talk about, my love," he says. "Today, why not call Aldous and have a tour of the kitchens or the gardens?"

"Tell me," I say.

He sighs, and adjusts his cuffs. His tailor has made sure that they land exactly on his wrist.

"There are men who believe I should be removed from power. Some of them wish me dead. This man is a leader of such a group."

I stop. What if it's Sylas? What if he's been captured just in the short time since I've seen him last? Or, if not Sylas, what if he's one of the men that Sylas trusts?

"You stay here and have a nice bath, or have Aldous have the kitchens make you a wonderful lunch, eh?" he says.

"These beautiful rooms begin to feel like a gilded cage," I say. "Why not let me come with you?" I ask.

"No," Olver says. "Out of the question."

"Why?" I ask. "I won't interfere. I'll stay far in the background."

"No," he says again and adjusts his tie. "Especially not today."

I hear the wiggle room.

"Please?" I ask. I walk to him and begin to adjust his tie and his jacket. "Please, my love?"

He sighs. He takes me hands into his.

"It will be gruesome. Ugly details about horrible men and their terrible lives," he says.

"But that sounds so much more interesting than having another bath or any tour."

He sighs again. "I shouldn't," he says.

I kiss him on the cheek. Then on the mouth. "Please?"

He sighs a third time, rolls his eyes, then smiles. "Fine," he says. "Get dressed."

After a long ride in the two-person travel pod, the courtroom seems enormous. The ceilings vault over us, the judges' desks feels as if they tower over us, even the doors are taller than a person. When I say something about it, Olver tells me it was all designed this way. Everyone is to feel small before the law.

"Aldous is waiting for you to communicate with him once you feel bored enough to go," Olver says. He's distracted from the moment we walk in to the room. "Stay toward the middle or back of the benches, please." He turns to leave.

"Wait," I say. "Aren't you staying?"

"I told you, beloved; today I am to act as part of the judging. I must sit up there," he says, pointing to the tallest part of the grouping of desks at the front of the room. "And I must go, because I need to get into my robes." He kisses me on the forehead, then on the mouth, and caresses my cheek, and then leaves.

Not long after he leaves, the room begins to fill up. One second there is no one in the room but me, and the next it feels cramped. After five minutes it feels crowded. I thought about moving to the front benches, but I can see that those are for the people who will be presenting their cases, and for the reporters. I keep peering at them trying to see if there are any I recognize from Sylas' group.

The low hum of conversation stops when two armed guards come in side doors at the front of the room. They place themselves between the benches and the judges' desks.

"All rise," one of them barks.

We all stand and then four men come in followed by a woman with a large data pad. She puts herself on the lowest set of desks. The men place themselves on the highest desks, but no one takes the center seat. Then Olver comes in.

I would be lying if I said his power in that moment wasn't attractive. The robes make him look like a god, something out of some ancient text, wrathful and wise. I find myself blushing, thinking about how I know the body under them so well.

"You may seat yourselves," Olver says and we all sit down.

There are many cases before we get to the one I'm concerned about, but I still don't see anyone from Sylas' group. I start to feel safe—perhaps the man they captured was someone new. Or maybe someone from a different part of the station entirely.

Then they call the next case and the side door, the one that one of the guards came through, opens. In walk two more guards with a young man who has the faint beginnings of a beard and tiny wire-rimmed glasses in a white jumpsuit. My jaw hits the floor—not only do I recognize him, he is one of Sylas' trusted men. Not a lieutenant, but on his way to being. They keep calling him by his prisoner number, but I know his name—Laro.

My pulse is pounding. I have to get out of here. I have to get off this planet. Can I make it to the shuttle port before men come to take me? Why haven't they done so already? If I remember right, Laro was even one of the men who came in through the passage and took me to Sylas once.

I'm dead.

Olver's men know everything. Which means that Olver knows everything. Or he soon will.

I'm missing the sentencing details because all I can hear is my heart slamming against my insides. I wonder if anyone else can hear it, too. They must be able to.

I have to get out of this room.

I have to get to Sylas. To warn him that they have Laro. Then maybe he can get me off this station and beyond Olver's reach. We can run together.

I stand up to leave.

Unfortunately, it is during a particularly quiet moment in the trial. When I stand, many people turn to look at me.

Including Laro.

And Olver.

I move to the aisle, convinced that everyone in the room can hear the pounding of my heart.

Once I'm outside, I realize I haven't been breathing.

I click the communicator and tell Aldous that I'd like for him to send the pod, that I'm not feeling well at all. He says it will be there in fifteen minutes. I start to say to him that's too long, that I have to get out now, but I stop myself. I tell him that will be fine.

I start to do the math. If I can get back to the palace and get through the tunnels fast enough to one of the places that I know Sylas' group tends to be, I can warn them and then I could maybe make it offworld in just over an hour. Is that enough time?

Will there be guards already in the pod when it arrives?

What are they waiting for?

Why haven't they taken me already?

I go to the pod hatch and wait. It is agonizing.

I would like to say that I spent the time thinking about how that young man was without a doubt going to be sentenced to death for trying to stand up to what he believed to be tyranny. I would love to say that I was the kind of person who was thinking about how noble that level of sacrifice could be.

Instead, when the pod arrives and I fold myself into it, all I'm thinking is that Olver must already know about me.

The pod door closes and with an almost imperceptible whoosh, I am on my way back to the palace.

# THE PAST

It is possible to just completely disappear from the lives of people who know you. I learned that fairly early on. I was picked up in a bar by a man who said he had connections. That he could get me into movies.

Just because it's one of the oldest lies in the universe doesn't mean that people don't still fall for it.

I was just dumb enough to think that this was my ticket out. Back then, I still trusted that there could be decent people. Back then, I was still young enough that I didn't keep a good watch on my drink. I woke up in a van a few hours later surrounded by other boys about my age. We were all tied and gagged and packed in tight enough that when the van would take a corner we didn't slide at all.

Eventually the van came to a stop and we were slid out onto carts one by one. We were loaded onto the floor of the cargo bay of a small shuttle. The entire time the crew that handled us were entirely silent. I didn't get a good look at them until after we'd already lifted off, but they were boys about our age, only their hair was shaved off and they all had these blank expressions. They strapped themselves in to benches that ran along the side of the cargo bay and said nothing as the shuttle's engines spun up and we lifted off. I wasn't the only one that was pleading with them to let us loose, to help us. They stared but their faces never moved.

Hours and hours later the shuttle descended and after a while the crew of boys along the wall undid their harnesses. The back of the shuttle opened and they slid us out one by one, lining us up shoulder to shoulder on our backs onto the deck. Nothing was moving around us so we all heard the boots of the man we would come to know as Veech. He was a sweaty, barrel-chested monster of a man in all black and red leather. As soon as he came to a stop, the crew of boys that had been handling us all went to their knees.

"So, my lads, you find yourself here. Not the worst place in the universe to be, but not where you thought you'd wind up, I'm sure." Veech put his hands on his hips. Then he pointed to one of us bound boys on the far end. "That one," Veech said. Two of the shaved headed boys stood and brought the boy Veech had pointed at to his feet. "To make sure I have your undivided attention," Veech said, then he walked over to the boy he'd pointed at. He took something out of his pocket and pointed it at the boy's head. There was a horrifying splat and blood exploded from the back of the boy's head. The two who had held him up let him drop to the deck. Their facial expressions never changed.

"Your only value from this day forward is in doing what I tell you to do. And that will be to work. You will work when you are told to without so much as a peep of protest or..." he said, and gestured toward the corpse on the deck. The boy lying next to me began to cry. "Do I make myself clear?" We were all still gagged but we answered as best we could. "Splendid. Take that away," Veech said. The boys who had been holding the corpse up grabbed it under the arms and dragged it away leaving a long trail of blood behind. "My name is Octobrius Veejarandanan. You will call me Veech. From this point forward, I control you."

And he did. Over the next few days we were shown what our job would be—harvesting rice from the almost festering pools of waist deep water where it was grown on a station that I never did learn the name of. "You can teach a machine to do an awful lot," Veech said, standing over us with the device that had destroyed the young man when we first arrived in his hand at all times. "But you can't, no matter how hard you try, make one that is as good as a young pair of hands at getting every last kernel without damaging the plant."

I won't bore you with all the details of the next year of my life because it fits into all the standard clichés you'd expect. When I think back on it, that's what hurts the most, I think…that I became a stupid cliché of suffering and defeat. I was not noble. I didn't attempt to lead a rebellion. I did not come to another boy's rescue from being assaulted by a guard or by Veech, himself. I kept my head down and did what I was told to do and I didn't resist when any of the guards decided I was what they wanted that night.

Sometimes the bravest thing you can do is to just keep on living.

The stories the others told made me feel sad; not just for those of us who were in the situation, but as over the top as it sounds, for humanity, itself. Up to that point, I'd never really thought about it, but I had a general feeling that life, the fact that something was living and breathing, was somehow important. It became very apparent that was not the case. One boy there, only a little older than me, said he'd been sold from operation like this to operation like this so many times he'd lost count. "Station, unregistered island, undersea platform, it doesn't matter anymore. I just do what they tell me," he said one night. Another, a huge-shouldered boy with a tiny waist from being starved like the rest of us, said that he was just glad to be alive—he'd been bought from a group that trained children to fight in pits for men to bet on. He'd only barely won the few matches he'd had and the men felt it better to try to make at least some money off him before he inevitably died. At night I could hear him crying. When I asked why, he said he could remember

161

the others he'd killed, that he never wanted to hurt them, but that he knew it was his life or theirs.

Orphans from countries that had outlawed abortion and quickly grown overpopulated, other kids who had to turn to crime to keep their younger siblings fed when their parents were killed or deported, also those who had learned, like me, that they could rent their bodies to others for an hour or so to make money for food, we were all there, etcetera. Those who were combinations of the above. It almost became boring, the stories were so similar. We had all found ourselves outside the protection of the law or the goodwill of the powers that be and were easily swept up by the predators that patrol society's boundaries for exactly that kind of prey.

Rescue, if you can call it that, only came after the sector government discovered that Veech's boss, a man whose name I never came to know, had been holding back his expected tax contribution from the rice farm. He was taken in and put on trial. Men in uniforms raided the farm and there was a firefight. Veech was killed along with most of the men who'd run the place. A few were left alive to be put on trial, I heard, but no one of any real importance. We were rounded up, taken back to Earth, given new clothes, fed, and given places to sleep. There were news stories about those of us. At first, they called us the "The Rice Slaves" which eventually faded to just Riceboys. I never listened to or read any of them, and I was never interviewed, but I heard about what was happening. The trial happened, the few who'd been caught were given sentences that seemed too small for what they'd done; at no point did they reveal the names of those higher up in their organization. There was public outcry. One by one they were eventually killed in various circumstances in jails. Eventually, like all things, no matter how horrifying, we faded from the public's attention. The number of cameras that would show up daily dwindled. The promises of housing and education dried up quickly once the spotlight was gone.

Just a year and a half after I'd been taken off them, I found myself back on the streets.

# SYLAS

I tap the wall near where the opening is with the pattern they told me to use if there was an emergency. Waiting for someone to come open the door is agonizing. The minutes tick by and I keep waiting for a servant to come in and tell me it's time for a bath or a nail clipping or some other interruption that will mean that I can't get to Sylas and warn him about Laro.

When it finally opens, I rush past the man into the tunnel saying, "I need to warn Sylas now," before he can say anything. I'm halfway down the tunnel to one of the stairways before I realize I don't know where Sylas might be. I stop and the man behind me squeezes past.

From the amount of time we're taking in the tunnels, I know Sylas must have been somewhere near the outer shell of the colony. I'm taken up through a street grating and into a tiny house. The woman who opens the door looks familiar but I can't place her name. She says something to the person who is leading me and he responds with a word. She closes the door and takes us back into the last room down the hallway.

Sylas sits on the floor looking at a data pad.

"Ah, you—"

Before he can get any further, "They have Laro. He saw me in court. They're going to get everything. They'll know about me, about you, about—"

"We will take tea, please," he asks and behind me the door closes.

He reaches across the small table and puts his hand on my shoulder. "You look exhausted." It stops me dead in my tracks. I realize two things in that moment—how incredibly attractive he is, and how tired I am. I sit down heavy on the cushion.

"I rushed right here. I needed to tell you," I say.

He nods and squeezes my shoulder. "You are very good to me."

"When did you…?" I start to panic; I want to tell him to run, that we have no time. The tea service comes in. Sylas takes time making the tea for both of us. There is something not only soothing about it, but again I'm struck by just how powerful he is, how in control of his actions. How much I want him.

"I know about Laro. I know we may seem like a fly by night kind of operation, but we are quite organized. A simple headcount after that raid and we knew who they had and what that might mean." Sylas hands me a cup of tea. It smells slightly of pepper and comfort. "Here," he says. He takes a sip from his own.

"Then…?" I don't even know what it is I want to ask, only that his calm doesn't feel like it fits.

He cocks his head to the side. "Laro knows quite a bit about the first level of our organization. It's unfortunate that they have him because it means that everything that level was doing will have to be halted and changed. We had just worked out many of the issues and it was running efficiently. Still, though, he only knew that level."

"Levels?" I ask.

"Yes, levels," Sylas says and sips from his tea again. "As with any organization, we have many parts doing many things. Again, I know we must seem very…how would you put it? Earnest but disorganized, like so many revolutions. However, that is not the case. Please don't be offended, but you think that because that is…well…what you have been allowed to see."

There is a knock at the door and the young man who brought me here enters. He hands a data pad to Sylas then leaves. Sylas glances over it for a moment then sets it aside.

"What I've been allowed to see?" I ask.

"Come, now. I like you very much," Sylas says, "but what reason would I have to show you every aspect of what I'm trying to do here?"

"But Laro saw me. He knows who I am," I say.

"And who are you?" Sylas asks with a grin.

"I…"

"What he knows is that someone he has seen before, whose name he does not know, appeared in court. I'm assuming that our great and powerful leader, long may he reign, left you in the audience box while he, himself, ascended to the grand throne of the courtroom?"

I nod.

"Olver has communicated your presence to very few outside the palace. The servants have seen you and know who you are, but they are all our people," Sylas says. I am taken aback. "Some soldiers have seen you during the tours, but many of them are either our people or in-debted to us for one reason or another. We even have people in his elite corps of questioners. Not as many as I'd like, but…" Sylas says.

"Then…" I say but don't know how to finish.

Sylas nods. "The situation is not quite as dire as you had thought." Sylas finishes his tea in one shot. He then leans forward and takes mine from me. He moves the table to the side of the room and sets my cup on it. Then he grabs me by the front of my shirt and pulls me to him.

Within a few seconds we are both undressed and tangled around one another. I lose myself in his hands and his lips, in his power.

After, when our breathing calms, he pulls me to him.

"Better?" he asks.

I do feel much more calm. I nod against his chest.

"Good," he says. "Unfortunately, you'll have to go soon."

"Let me stay," I say. "There's no reason for me to go back to him. Let me stay and help. Besides, he might know."

"He's suspected you for some time," Sylas says.

I sit up. "What?"

"Calm yourself, my love, calm yourself," Sylas says. "He suspects everyone."

"But you said earlier…"

"That even if my men can't make sure to be the ones questioning Laro, even if they are Olver's men and even if Laro does wind up giving you up, what does he really have to tell?"

"But if Olver knows…"

"I said he was suspicious. He doesn't *know* anything. It would be prudent to keep playing the game the way we have been. That means that you must go back," Silas says.

"But why?"

He sighs. "Because it is likely that you will have to be the one to shoot him."

I sit up on my elbow. "What?"

"You are beautiful when you are incredulous," Sylas says running his hand along my jaw, down my neck, along my shoulder.

"Tell me what you mean," I say.

He looks at me for a moment and I have to remember that I'm somewhat mad rather than kiss him.

"You must go back to the palace because you are part of the plan. A vital part."

"What does that mean?"

"As I said—there are many aspects to the organization, and there are many layers to the plan. You are a part of that plan just as much as the second clone is," Sylas says.

There is another knock at the door. The young man from before enters with another data pad. He hands it to Sylas and waits. Sylas looks it over, then looks back at the young man and nods. The young soldier takes the pad back and leaves.

"What part of the plan am I?" I ask.

"Perhaps we should talk about it some other time," he says.

"No, let's talk about it now," I say.

He lies back down.

He looks at me for a moment, then pulls me closer.

"The truth?" he asks.

"Of course," I say.

"We saw an opportunity. We intercepted the communications packet that said you'd be arriving and we saw an opening," Sylas says.

For a second, I'm drawn aback by the blatant truth of it. From the beginning, the plan had been to use me to get to Olver.

"We had to scramble, though. His initial communication with you wasn't intercepted for some reason. We didn't know until you were already en route."

"It was a letter," I say.

"What?"

"It was a letter. He handwrote it. To me. That's why you didn't intercept it through your listening programs. He handwrote a letter and had it shipped," I say.

Sylas shakes his head slowly. "The cost must have been staggering."

"I think that was the point," I say. "I think he wanted me to see what lengths he was willing to go to in order to...to get my attention."

"It worked," Sylas says. "But how...?"

"I know. The time dilation. I have no idea. I keep wanting to ask him about it, but then I get...distracted," I say. I pause for a second, wondering if I've said too much; if I've hurt him by revealing any of this.

He kisses the top of my head.

"You were a blessing from God, for whom all things are possible."

"Was there...?" I start but stop.

"Was there what, beloved?" Sylas asks.

"Olver. Did he...did he have someone before me?"

Quiet settles over us.

"When he was younger. A lieutenant of his. The...sect...that most of his supporters come from believe that for men to have such relations with one another is wrong. It's still done, of course, but it has to be kept very secret. He and his...friend... were able to keep it secret for quite a while. Unfortunately, the lieutenant was killed in one of the few skirmishes that sometimes happen with Olver's off the books shipments. He stayed alone for a long time, grieving. We all thought perhaps he would never recover, but then...you," Sylas says.

"And the one you come from?" I ask.

"My family and the families that lived around us were always much more of the opinion that happiness is what God would want. That if two young men find happiness with one another, find joy and love with each other, then that must be just as much the will of God as anything else that happens."

I snuggle further into his arms.

"What is it you will need me to do," I ask.

He kisses my forehead. The gesture is so tender, so mild, that I tear up a bit.

"So long as he has the mobile armor suits, we cannot defeat him,"

Sylas says. "No matter how close we get to him, we cannot get anyone into the pilot corps. There is a psychological test the pilots all must take. They say it is to make sure they will synchronize well with the robots, but…" he sighs.

"But?" I ask.

"I suspect it is a loyalty test. This is why none of our candidates have ever passed it. So we cannot get in legitimately, and we dare not kill one of them to replace them."

"Why not?" I ask.

"The suit is keyed to the pilot through a code. Once we have one of the codes, my men assure me we can crack those codes and then gain control of many if not all of the mobile suits. Still, though…"

"You need at least one of the codes," I say.

"We need at least one of the codes," he repeats. "And he has been showing you how to pilot one, has he not?"

I sigh. "Okay," I say. "I'll get you a code."

I can feel him smile. I know I've been lead to this by him—I'm not a fool. But I *want* to be lead. I want to be the only one who can accomplish something for him.

"But there's more, isn't there?" I ask, finally giving voice to what I have felt for a while now.

"There is," Sylas says.

"What is it?" I ask.

"We may need you to be an even bigger part of the plan if things go…badly," Sylas says.

The quiet stretches out between us.

"What will you need me to do?" I ask. I already know. I've known for a long time now.

"I think you already know," he whispers.

"You want me to kill Olver."

"At some point it may become necessary for you to do so. If it does, there will be a time when you will be alone with him. In that moment, you would use a gun we will give to you."

"How will I know?"

"When it is time?" Sylas asks. "You will know. Let us hope, though, that it does not become necessary. There is still another part of the plan that will be tried first."

Could I really do it? After all, even after hearing the things that Olver was guilty of, I didn't hate him. He had never spoken a harsh word to me. In fact, we had always with a closeness, an openness that I had never experienced before…except for with Sylas. It was never love, but then again, it was never hate, either. I'd even grown fond of him.

Could I kill him?

"What would you have done if I had arrived and was not willing to help?" I ask.

"So you are not mad? You *are* willing to help?" Sylas asks.

"What would you have done if I wasn't?" I ask.

"Let's not think about that."

"It's okay; tell me."

Sylas leans his cheek against the top of my head. "I am very happy that was not the case," he says, confirming what I had already thought. "However, on some level you are right to want to be cautious. Perhaps we have less time than I had initially wanted. We may need to move faster."

"What makes you say that?" I ask.

"That report I just received. Laro did not give you up to the questioners who were, unfortunately, not our men. However, he did give up the location of one of our cloning stations. An important one, as it turns out."

"So what does that mean?" I ask as we are both getting dressed.

"There was a raid just moments ago on the station where we were developing the second clone. It has been destroyed."

"But then…then the plan is off. Olver knows!" I begin to panic.

"There was just enough time for the soldiers there to…erase the clone's face," Sylas says putting his last boot on.

"But the DNA," I say.

"Yes, they will test its DNA and discover who it is meant to be. The good news is that takes time. The bad news is that this means the first clone will have to be put into play. A terrible choice to make, but the only one that leaves us still capable of making the correct date."

The second he says it, my mind goes to the same place his is.

"Salil," I say.

He nods.

Then it's my turn to sigh heavily.

"They tell me that, barring anything unforeseen, even a clone that has been decanted as long as he has can still be put back in and accelerated to the correct age. There will be some…complications, however."

"Like?" I ask.

"The brain in such cases loses all memory that was already stored in favor of the maturated cell structure. Unlike simply growing older, where the brain would retain older memory and simply store new memory, the maturated brain overwrites the old cell structures," Sylas says. "He will lose everything that he is. The ultimate sacrifice for our cause. I had…I had gotten used to the idea that he would be…that perhaps he might be my son."

I get my second shoe on and then we are both fully dressed, as if our time together hadn't happened. It makes me sad that it can be erased so quickly, so easily. Sylas walks out of the room and I follow. The young soldier meets us at the door and we quick march to the nearby tube entrance.

Once inside, Sylas punches in the code that I know means he's disabled the surveillance systems. The second code changes the pod over to manual control. He then presses the launch button and we're pushed back in our seats.

"This will be horrible for him," I say. The lights of the tube flash past us so quickly that they almost look like one continuous beam.

"He will survive," Sylas says.

"Of course he'll survive, I'm just…right now, these are the last minutes of his life as he knew it, as he expected it to be, and he doesn't even know. The minute we walk in the door, his life is over."

Sylas says nothing for a long time.

"I was five when my mother was taken for 'questioning.' My father had been part of the resistance, but my mother…I didn't know what was happening at the time, but when I later became part of the resistance, I went back through all the records that had been kept. She knew nothing. Those that were involved at the time had begged my father to bring her in. She had a knack for chemistry, it seems. But he refused. All of them noted in their own ways that he refused to bring her in or even tell her about what he was doing. Still, Olver's father's dogs…they killed her. I was left alone. I existed on the streets for a time, but eventually I was bought," Sylas said, making quote motions with his fingers. "At first for my tenacity. There were no dogs for dog fighting pits, so they used street children. I was a favorite because I would win in…horrible…ways. I never knew. I just blacked out and then came to later. It was a drug they would shoot into our veins." Sylas sighs. I want to reach over and put my hand on his arm, but I can't. Such a tiny distance, but it seems as uncrossable as an ocean. "When I started to grow, though, It didn't escape the notice of those who were fond of boys. There was, it seems, an entire subculture of people who not only enjoyed watching children tear each other apart viciously, but also wanted to have sex with the victors. The first time, I wasn't even told what was happening. I was simply told to go with this particular man. I'd seen him before, always in the company of the doctor that was used after fights to patch me back together for the next one. I thought I was just going for another bandage or shot of vitamins to keep me well enough to win. He told me that he was going to be giving me the vitamin shot, but instead he drugged me, and when I woke up, my body slowly came to and I realized what must have happened. Those pains are…unmistakable. For a while, he was the only one who would…purchase me. But as I grew more and more victorious, others paid more attention. It wasn't long before the man who was running things simply told me what was happening, and what was to happen next. So I would spend part of my days training to win fights, and then most nights being used in whatever manner had been paid for." He doesn't say anything for a bit. I want to look over at him but I know he wants nothing more than to not be looked at. "It's ironic in many ways—I was capable of fending them off, but I didn't care too, even though I hated what was happening. I thought about it…how I would crush their windpipe or break an elbow…but where would I run? Where could I possibly go? The…'care' of the man who owned me and his men were all I'd ever really known."

"How did you get away?" I ask.

"Eventually I grew into a man's body and that not only disqualified me from being their prize fighter, but also from being an object of…

affection…for many of the men involved. Our culture is quite specific about the ways that men may interact with one another, but somewhat less so when it comes to men and boys." Sylas says. After a moment, he says, "and the resistance was there, ready to scoop me up. They had been watching for some time, you see, ready to take in the young men who were now trained fighters but had been set adrift. Still, as calculated as it all could be, I will never be able to repay my debt to them."

"Did you stop the practice once you came to power?" I ask.

"I would have, but I didn't have to. The man who was our leader just before me, who had been a young man when I was first recruited; he had come through the same…situation. He took care of it before I became even a lieutenant. He made it his mission to clean up the black market and make it work for the resistance. Once I inherited control, the black market was already fully integrated as an arm of the resistance movement. The type of boys who used to be easy prey for monsters like the ones I encountered are now brought in to the resistance from the start…given shelter, fed, cared for, trained."

"Trained to do what?" I ask.

"Each according to his or her own gifts. Some are good at cooking, some at cleaning, some at fighting, some at overhearing things…"

"Child soldiers," I say out loud before I can stop myself. I look over at Sylas to see his reaction.

He breaks into a smile, "for the cause of their own liberation, yes." He turns to me and puts his hand on my shoulder. "I know how it must sound to you. I truly do. But consider the alternative. None of them will ever have to endure what I endured. They can look on their time with us proudly and say that they gave their all for the cause of freedom from tyranny. What better childhood could one have?"

The music is loud as we enter the hallway. Before we even reach the room, I know what we will find. Sylas pushes through the door and inside, the little man is going through a series of twirls, leaping through the air. Sylas nods to the two men next to the door and they salute and leave. He glances at me, letting me know that I can leave if I choose. I stay, though. Something in me feels I owe the boy this.

Sylas makes a few gestures letting the room know that he would like the music turned off. It fades and then disappears. The boy stops and turns to face us, seeing us for the first time. He runs to Sylas and they hug.

"Did you see?" he asks.

"I did! You leap like a young deer."

"What's a deer?" Salil asks. My heart breaks.

"A kind of large mammal from the homeworld of long ago. We don't have them here because there isn't enough woodland space for them to survive in any significant numbers," Sylas says. The boy's eyes flicker to me and then back to Sylas and I see the love, the unbridled trust in them. "Go and get cleaned up and change. We must talk."

The boy leaves to shower and it's a mercy. His dance leotards do nothing but show how tiny, how frail his body is. To think of putting such a creature into harm's way makes me feel like a monster. Sylas and I sit on the lip of the small stage at the far side of the room. The boy returns in regular street clothes. He still seems far too small for the burden we are to deliver, but perhaps a little less so.

"Come and sit by us," Sylas says patting the stage next to him.

"Have I done something wrong?" Salil asks as he sits.

"Nothing could be further from the reason why we are here," Sylas says. He puts his arm around the boy's shoulders. "As I have told you before, you were born to a great purpose. Do you remember?"

"Yes," Salil says.

"And do you remember how I told you that one day, it might come to pass that you might be asked to fulfill that purpose?"

"You said it would bring great glory to my name," Salil says. I can not only hear the rote memorization in the response, I can also hear the beginnings of worry.

"Today, my son, is that day."

I see Salil's eyes light.

"Things have come to pass that require we now burden you with a great task. Your name will go down in the rolls of those who have given all for the revolution."

The boy smiles and there is nothing but happiness behind it.

"However, with such glory comes great sacrifice," Sylas says.

"What sacrifice?" Salil asks.

Sylas sighs. "Tomorrow, a man will come to collect you and take you to a machine. That machine will make you a man because it is you as a man that we require for our plan to work."

Salil says nothing. "Will it hurt?"

"I wish I could tell you that it wouldn't, but it will. This is part of the sacrifice we are asking you to make," Sylas says. "However, I have seen your great heart, and I know that you can bear such a minor thing as pain."

"What will happen then?" Salil asks.

"You will be trained to kill a man."

"Will I be able to dance, still?" Salil asks.

Sylas shakes his head. "This training must happen very quickly—day and night it will be. I'm afraid that you will not have time to dance anymore."

Salil begins to cry. I see him try to fight the tears back but he cannot. The resulting scene destroys me. I begin to weep silently myself.

"But it makes me happy," Salil says.

"And it made me happy. However, now is the time to put away the things of childhood. You must fulfill the glorious purpose for which you were created."

"But you said someone else would do that," Salil says, his voice nearly breaking.

"Had things gone well, he would have. However, the other one like you, the one who was to carry this burden, he was found and destroyed this morning," Sylas says.

"…please…" Salil begs almost too quiet to hear.

Sylas pulls him closer. "If there was some other way, any other way, I would spare you this. However, there is not. It is a task only you can complete."

"…someone else…" Salil whispers through tears.

"Your name will go down in the rolls of those without whom no freedom could ever have been achieved," Sylas says. He kisses the top of the boy's head and stands. He signals me to follow. We walk out, leaving the boy there to cry by himself in the big, empty, quiet room.

Days later.

The gun shakes.

"I'm uncomfortable," I say.

Sylas slips in behind me, his arm along my arms, his hand underneath my wrists.

"Relax," he says. "Breathe."

"I am breathing," I say.

"Not the way that I showed you." He makes a show of inhaling loudly and exhaling loudly. I feel his breath against my neck.

I close my eyes and settle back into him. I inhale and exhale.

The gun stops shaking.

"Again. Remember, down into your gut," Sylas says.

I inhale, trying to picture drawing the breath going all the way down into my feet. Then I exhale, pushing a bit with my diaphragm.

"Good. Once more," Sylas whispers.

I do.

"Good," he says. "Remember, if something goes wrong, and you have to be the one to do this, then at the moment we most need you, there will be a lot of adrenaline pumping through you."

"I know," I say. I start to think about the first time I was on camera. The lights. The people all around. I push that thought away. "And I might not even have to do it," I say.

"That is correct," Sylas says. "All of this training might be for nothing."

"Now, as I showed you before. One eye open, one closed. Sight down your arm. Think of the barrel of the gun as just an extension of your will. Aim with your heart," he says. He's said the same thing every time we've done this. I've lost count of how many times we've been down here, in the abandoned section, practicing shooting.

"Get comfortable," he says. "The more tense you are, the more likely the weapon will do something you don't want it to." He inhales and exhales, then pulls the trigger with my finger around it. The gun barks once.

"He always carries a pistol just like this one," Sylas says. He lets go a bit, backing up a step. "If we have to rely on you, you will already know this gun before you even have to pull it from its holster on his hip."

Ten times? Fifteen? I truly have lost count of how often we've been down here. I remember for a moment the first time. Even holding the gun by myself was difficult. I thought myself so powerful, that I had done so much in my life. What's a gun? I had thought. I had stood naked, erect, what would normally be a very vulnerable moment, in front of hundreds of people at live sex shows and conventions without thinking myself helpless, or exposed, for even a moment.

But holding the pistol, knowing the lethal force it carries, changes the way I felt about myself.

"Again," Sylas says as he has so many times.

I go back through the checklist: plant feet, bend knees slightly, bend elbows slightly, breathe in, breathe out, squeeze trigger. The gun howls again.

"Again," Sylas says.

I run the checklist. The gun erupts.

"Again," Sylas says.

Checklist. The gun barks.

I expect him to say "again" once more, but instead he's unzipping my pants. In moments we're naked and it's all power and clutching and primal, a garden of lower brain delights. With him inside of me, I feel powerful, capable of anything. I see the gun and I feel lethal. I pull away from Sylas and before he knows what's happening, I take him from behind for the first time.

When I explode, it is as close as I've ever gotten to the first time.

Lying next to one another, he watches me as though I am something new, some strange and terrible creature he has found himself too close to.

"It has been a very long time since..." he whispers. I pull close to him and slide into his arms. I can feel him relax as the universe returns to making sense. He pulls me closer.

"The time is coming soon," I say. I feel him nod. "When will we know if the clone is going to be ready?"

"I will," I say. "I will. But I have a question."

"What is it?" he asks.

I aim. Center. Fire again. Closer this time.

"If so many of the people around him are yours, then why do you need anyone to do this? Why not just have one of them slip something into his food? Or kill the oxygen to his bedchamber while he sleeps?" I ask without looking at him. To be honest, I'm ashamed that it's taken me this long to think of it, then longer to ask. It was only after I considered what we had done to Salil that I began to even wonder.

"There are two reasons," he says. "One is that, as much as I hate to admit it, we haven't been able to get people into the *right* positions. We have people all around him, all throughout his organization, but none of them where it counts. No key holders, if you see what I mean."

He sighs and looks away. "It would have solved so many different problems. But..." he looks back at me. I lower the gun. "The other is that I want this all to at least appear legal. There are those, not just away from the station, but here on the station itself, who are...not neutral to be sure, but at least not directly involved in the effort to overthrow... him."

"Hence the need for the clone," I say.

"Hence the need for the clone," he repeats. "It isn't the ones who are directly against us that we must worry most about, but those who have made their peace with the current way of things. The ones who would never think of revolution as the answer to anything. We must find a way to keep them..."

"Unaware?" I ask.

He nods. "Unaware."

I nod, turn back to the target, breathe deep, aim, and fire. Closer, always closer to the bullseye.

# THE PAST

One company I auditioned for really liked me and wanted me to do several videos for them in a row. The owner of the place naturally wanted to have sex with me, too, but that's pretty much included in the deal for someone who is new to the business.

We're still just meat to be passed around at a feast until we have a name. *Then* we can say no.

During the first video, I started to notice that there are a lot of impossibly young looking guys hanging around the set. Back then, I didn't know what a crew looked like. Now, I would be immediately alarmed. Teamsters are teamsters no matter what year is on the calendar.

I can't help but notice, too, that they only ever talk to each other. On breaks, they are only ever together, their heads bowed toward each other, one of them eyeing the rest of us to make sure that we don't come too close. It's especially noticeable when we have a meal break (for all of the owner's skeeviness, he was at least aware that he needed to run the set in a similar way to an actual movie set or else someone was likely to talk to someone who would talk to someone which always leads to a 3 a.m. raid, eventually).

When we're all trying to choke down the underdone spaghetti served from a crock pot, all of them huddle together talking and not eating. It was fairly easy to spot them because they all looked like one another. White t-shirts with no graphics on them, jeans that were usually two sizes too big and obviously about to fall apart (so definitely from the thrift store), the same third or fourth-hand canvas sneakers. They were all either naturally blonde or very obvious bottle jobs.

There was something distinctively…rat-like is the only word I have ever been able to come up with…about their faces. Sharp angles. Front teeth barely hidden by upper lip. That kind of thing.

At any rate, there were a few of them on the first shoot.

Then a few more on the second.

By the third shoot, the whole crew were these guys.

I started to notice, too, that they won't look at me while we're filming. Again, at the time, I wasn't aware of how unusual that was. During filming, even a straight guy holding the overhead microphone pole watches what's happening on set so that he can make sure the microphone isn't in the shot (the owner makes decent money off these films, but no way does he have enough to get even one drone camera, let alone enough to replace a crew, so he does things the old fashioned way). And out of what could be active or simply bored curiosity. No matter what their motivation is, they watch.

These guys wouldn't, though. They look up, they look to the side; they look everywhere they possibly can except at me getting sucked off, or me getting plowed, and they especially don't look while the other performers are licking my feet (this particular company is known for making films where that kind of thing is expected).

After a fairly light day of shooting on the third film, I happened to bump in to one of these guys while I'm on the way to the table to get myself a doughnut. I was thinking about what I needed to do with the money once the next check was in the bank, in a completely different mindspace, and suddenly there he was. Then we're both on the ground.

"I'm sorry," I said, sitting up.

He says nothing but simply stares at me as if I've caught fire. I stand up and offer him my hand to help him up, but he just stares at me, his eyes huge. It was as if he was trying to hold in a scream.

One of the other lookalike boys came over and helped him up, and immediately they bent their heads together, talking. I stood there for a minute, wondering if they were going to say anything to me at all, but all they do is glance at me for a second, then go back to whispering. They stopped whispering, and the one that came over to help the first one up puts his arm around the guy, and they walked away.

Later, after we're done shooting for the day, I scrub myself down with some wipes (no way we can afford trailers, let alone trailers with showers), just to get clean enough to put clothes on and go home where I can soak in a hot tub for a while. The door to the back room we've been using opens.

"Occupied," I said without looking up. It was a fairly common occurrence for people to just open doors and walk in—they'd all already seen everything us performers had to show, so there was no attempt at modesty.

The door closed and there was the kid I'd bumped in to.

"You need to come with me," he said.

"I what?" I asked. I noticed at that moment that he was looking at me, and at that same moment I noticed that he had light blue eyes, the kind that aren't pretty but instead alarming.

"You need to come with me," he said. The door opened again and another one of them came in. This one was taller than the first, and as soon as he closed the door behind him, he *looked* at me with dark green eyes. I can't even begin to describe how unsettling it was to suddenly have two of them who had spent the better part of a year not looking anywhere near me to suddenly have their eyes directly on me.

They're about to kidnap you, some part of me said to myself.

I laughed it off, though. I started to get dressed.

Another one came in and closed the door behind himself. This one not as tall as the second, and with brown eyes.

"Look, fellas," I said. "If you want to have a party, I'm okay with that, just let me get dressed and tell me where we're going." I have to admit that, even though this felt all kinds of off, I was curious.

They looked at each other then back at me in one motion. I couldn't help but think about horror movies I'd seen.

"To see Him," the first one said. I could hear the capital letter.

I shouldn't have, but I agreed to go. I had to know more about this story.

As it turned out, they all lived together in this huge old farmhouse way up in the hills. If it was a working farm or just a conveniently big plot of land away from prying eyes, I never really knew. As it also turned out, I wasn't imagining things—they all did dress alike in the exact same thrift and hand-me-down clothes and shoes, and they were all blonde (either naturally or made to be that way).

If any of them had a name, I can't say I remember hearing it.

The ride up to the house was completely silent except for the shorter one with the disquieting blue eyes saying, "I think he's going to really like you."

I caught sight of myself in one of the car's outside mirrors and noticed for the first time how much I sort of looked like them. By midsummer, my hair would be light enough that from a distance, we could be twins.

They took me across the farm to a small building near the fence line. There we waited, though not very long, until the door opened and a man walked in flanked by two more boys. These were decidedly younger than the ones that I'd seen. He was about the same height as me, with curly brown hair and dark green eyes that he kept behind glasses. He was dressed in fairly modern clothes, though, and I couldn't help but notice that his shoes were expensive.

"Hello," he said. I noticed the same flat-voice, lack-of-accent that they all seemed to have, too. Like an anchor on a national news program.

"Hi," I said.

He made a gesture and they boys brought folding chairs over, opened them for us, then went back to standing near the wall.

"This is a cult, isn't it?" I asked and laughed nervously.

He said, "we don't like that word. It has such an ugly history." He cocked his head to the side. "This is a place of shelter for people who need it. A place of comfort for those who will accept it. That's all." He extended his flat palms out facing upward and the boys around the wall all bowed their heads and muttered something.

Even then, for some reason, though I could tell there might be danger here, I didn't feel as if I was in any.

That's how I came to meet The Sons of Aram.

You remember the name.

Yes, I mean *those* Sons of Aram.

So you know how this turns out in the end. However, let me tell you how it turned out for *me*.

I knew that I could walk away at any point I wanted. They made that quite clear. The problem was, I didn't want to.

I mean, that's what you've been wondering. That's the question that's on everyone's mind when it comes to something like this. "Why didn't you just leave?" Trust me, those first two days, I wanted to. I thought about it.

But they were so…nice. I don't know how else to describe it. Everything about living there was like being in a bath where the water is the perfect temperature. Every time I turned around, someone was there to ask me how I was feeling, if I wanted something, touching me in a way that was not in the slightest way sexual—just warm and reassuring.

When I talked, they looked only at my eyes and truly *listened*.

Imagine that for a second. To be surrounded by people who are honestly listening when you say something.

After a bit, I found myself doing it, too. Listening when someone was saying something. Asking them questions about what they were saying instead of just waiting for my own turn to talk.

"Why the porn?" I asked the man I met that first day. For the first few days, all I knew him by was what they called him; Malachi. I thought that Malachi was the head of the group, but it turns out that he was just the guy who was in charge of new folks.

Like most new folks, I had been helping out in the kitchen when he came in. To my surprise, he rolled up his sleeves and started to help wash dishes with me.

"There are a lot of mouths to feed, here and, though we do grow our own crops, we find ourselves having a need for money. At least, for now. Here in the early phases of things," he said. "It's a business where there aren't a lot of questions asked."

"There isn't some…I don't know…commandment against sinning or something?" I asked.

He smiled. "This isn't that sort of group."

"You're aware that this is something that could be thought of as…"

"A cult?" he asked and laughed. "Yes." He took the last plate from me and dried it absently. Smiling, he said, "None of us are blind to what's going on, here. Not even Aram. Least of all him, as a matter of fact. But this isn't that kind of thing. We truly are just trying to build a place…a mindset…where people can heal." He didn't say anything for a moment, then put the dish into the drainer. "There were always things about those…cults…as people like to call them…things that they got right. Through Aram, we're finding our way. Keep the good things, reject the bad. You'll see." He said, squeezed my arm in a way that made me feel warm all over, and then left.

I was assigned to night meetings on Wednesdays and Saturdays. That first night happened to be a Wednesday, so it was on that first evening that I met Aram.

There had to be about a hundred of us all sitting in chairs that were brought out and assembled in a circle once the tables and long benches had been cleared away to the walls in the big building where we'd all just eaten dinner. While we'd been doing that, it was all calm and peaceful chatting. As soon as we all got seated, though, an electric quiet settled over the crowd. I found myself bouncing my knee in anticipation.

There's no other way for me to describe Aram other than he's exactly what I expected. Half Silicon Valley tech-geek stereotype with his tiny-rimmed glasses, and half strangely attractive whipcord thin model. A body that said he'd never once even considered going to a gym, but could do a hundred pull-ups without getting winded. Like almost everyone else (there were a few other new folks like me who hadn't changed yet), he wore a white t-shirt and jeans and canvas sneakers. His most striking feature, though, was his platinum blonde hair. Unlike the boys I'd first met or, indeed, most of the other people I'd seen in the group, his wasn't bleached; he had been born with silver hair and pale blue eyes.

"Friends," he said as soon as he reached the center of the circle. "It's very good to see you this evening. Let's all take a moment to thank

Aiden and the rest of the kitchen crew for that fantastic stew tonight," he said and clapped. The room erupted in applause. It died down after a few moments and he stood there smiling, looking around the room. I saw Malachi hanging out near the door. He smiled at me and I smiled back.

The positive energy in the room was something you could feel, physically, like an ocean, ebbing and surging.

"I see a lot of new faces," Aram said. His gaze swept over me and I found myself hoping he'd look again. "It's so very good to see you here, tonight. Remember, as always, that you are free to go. But I hope you will stay. We are stronger with you here."

"Stronger with you here," the crowd whispered. The hairs on the back of my neck stood up. When I asked if it was a good feeling or a bad feeling, I couldn't pry them apart.

"Stronger with you here," Aram repeated quietly, almost absently. When his gaze lighted on me once again for just a moment, I knew I wasn't going to leave. In his eyes was approval, and care.

"No matter what the path that has lead you to us here, we *are* stronger with you as one of us. And in the coming days and months, we will keep growing stronger as we learn from you and you learn from us. The world outside our little patch of ground, here, is cold. I know that," he said. I felt that he knew the things I had done, that had been done to me. "I know the kinds of things you've had to do to survive it. We all have. There is no judgment here. No shame. We are not the things we have to do sometimes, but instead we are something different. Something luminous. Something more than the crude matter that sits in these chairs."

Most of what he said that night, and what he said most nights, was this. A reminder to us all that we were stronger if we didn't judge each other, if we accepted one another and tried to help each other get through the day. A reminder that we were our higher selves, not the ones that had to punch keys on a cash register or hold an overhead microphone on a porn set.

Someone at the end of the talk on that first day asked, "why no women?"

They weren't being excluded, Aram said, but we as men needed some time away to work on ourselves if we were going to help make the world a better place. The world outside what he always called "our little patch of ground" had taught us to rape and beat and steal and burn. It was going to take some time for us to figure out what was really important so that we didn't do those things anymore. "There's no one else that can help us with that," Aram said, "but other men."

At the end of his talk that night, the room erupted in applause.

I didn't go back to the porn shoot the next day. Instead, I stuck around and helped with the tomatoes. The next day with the potatoes. By the end of that first week, I was listening more and saying less. By the end of the second week, I was sleeping all the way through the night, something I hadn't been able to do since I was seven. I met so many incredible young men, heard their stories, told my own, and we all marveled at how similar they sounded. I grew to care about them in a way I hadn't even felt with anyone else.

So much so that I never even bothered to ask why people bleached out their hair and cut it short. It was just something we all did to seem like the older ones, to seem like Aram.

Of course, though, you know the stories. You know how this goes.

Eventually one of the underage boys he was routinely having sex with, the ones that he was submitting to horrible torture that they were almost all brainwashed into wanting, into thinking that they were being somehow purified, escaped. The compound, which is what the outside world started calling it rather than "our little patch of land" was raided. They not only saved all the boys, but they also discovered his other plans—the huge tanks of poison gas that he was hiding away for the attack on the subway system. The documents he'd kept about all the poison attacks he'd already had young men, young men like me, carry out around the country.

It turns out that Malachi had been 100% wrong. The Sons of Aram were exactly like any and every other cult ever.

They always are.

In hindsight over those next few weeks, what I felt the most wasn't anger or betrayal. It was loss. I swear to you that I never saw any underground storage facilities filled with row upon row of gas tanks, that I never saw any of the young boys with bruises on their faces. He'd found a way to keep them separate from all of us from the second they got anywhere near the...the compound. All I ever saw were young men, guys like me, guys I worked beside, talked about my shitty life with, cared about.

After a week or so of talking with the FBI, I was released. I got back to the apartment I'd been living in a day before the notice on the door said they were going to kick me out. I got the bills caught up by almost emptying out my account. I found myself just sitting there, though, on that stupid little patio, staring across the hills. I thought about where those guys I cared so much for were now. Most of them probably weren't lucky enough to have some place to go.

The people in the industry were happy to see me again. I did a few movies in clothes that mimicked what we'd worn in the group. For a year after, the hottest thing were stories of fucking a cultist. Hot cultist on cultist action. Big dicked cultists initiating new members. All the little studios found a way to cash in. Then mainstream fashion kicked in and for a few months, everyone was bleached blonde and wearing thrift store clothes.

All I had to do was keep my hair bleached and wear the same worn-thin jeans with the hole in the knee and make myself sound like Malachi and I built up my bank account again. At first I kept wondering if someone was from the cult or not. I'd say things, little phrases, and see if they would respond. No one ever did, though. Eventually I stopped.

The next year, a different group was discovered up in the mountains of Wyoming. When the FBI went in there, it was a massacre. They discovered all the bodies had either dyed or naturally dark black hair and everyone was wearing a particular name brand sneaker.

I let my natural hair grow out.

I worked a little less.

# OLVER

"I want to ask you for something," I say.

Olver finishes sliding into his shirt and starts closing the buttons. "Oh?"

"The mobile armor suits," I say, "the mechs. You've shown me so much, I…I want to know more."

He stops buttoning his shirt and smiles at me. "I thought you might."

"I'd…I'd like to take one out on my own."

He nods. "And someday soon you will, my beloved." He finishes dressing.

"But," I say, "what if I wanted to do it soon? Maybe today?"

He grabs his hat from its stand.

"This excited, are you? Well, I can arrange that. I'll have General Waijen collect you and take you out with him on patrol of the docks."

I nod. "Thank you, my beloved," I say, standing up without putting any clothes on and wrapping my arms around him.

He kisses me deeply and smacks my ass. Then he puts on his hat. I straighten it for him. He turns on his heel and leaves.

A few hours later, the General comes to the door. I'm already dressed, but I wait for a few moments. He rings the bell once more. I walk very slowly up the stairs.

"I was told to collect you and bring you on patrol," he says. Without saying anything else, he turns on his heel and goes to the lift. I follow, but then start patting my pockets. "What is it?" he asks.

"My lucky medallion," I say. "I can't leave without it." I mime panic and rush back into the apartment.

My plan is to fake being such an imbecile that in his frustration, he gives the startup codes to me to use on my own rather than starting the mech for me. I can see already that it's working. I count to thirty and then emerge with relief on my face. We travel down to the hangar deck. He's already so late that all his men are loaded up in their mechs and in formation awaiting him. He's doing an admirable job hiding his frustration with me, but only barely.

"Do you know the startup code?" he asks. I delay answering until we're so close to his own mech that for him to walk all the way over to the one that sits pilotless, the one they've set aside for me, would make his patrol very late in starting.

"Startup code?" I ask.

His eye roll is enormous. "Can you remember this?" he asks and then rattles off a string of numbers to me. Without waiting to see what I say, he turns on his heel and moves into the cockpit of his own mobile suit. I walk as slowly as possible over to the lone pilotless one. Behind me, the thunderous clanking of the patrol moving to the rolling hangar door. I punch the code I was given into the keypad of the mech left out for me and the footholds extend from the spots they were stored flush with the robot's skin. I climb up inside and, already beginning the startup procedures as the cockpit door closes. Only when it's fully down do I allow myself to smile.

# THE PAST

The monks of St. George Michael the Immaculate were an interstellar group of party planners who would find a celestial body that was about to be destroyed and hold an enormous party on it. Asteroids on a collision course with one another, a proto-planet that was in a decaying orbit, what have you. The idea was that if you truly wanted to introduce the concept of impermanence and living in the now, there had to be an element of danger involved. Buddhism with a twist of lime, you might say.

I was invited to one of their more interesting affairs after my third movie, "All Boys School Planet 2" went viral throughout the inner core planets. We had done so much work on the plot line that some movie critic algorithms said this was the must-see film of that year. "I remember there being a lot of good feelings behind the camera on that set" was my standard line when reporters asked, but truthfully, I don't remember anything that happened on that shoot. Like so many other films, that set ran on uppers and vodka and the eternally renewable energy source of young males wanting attention from other young males.

At any rate, the monks of St. Georgies (meant to rhyme with "orgies" if you see it) had asked me to show up to what they were calling "A Balls." Like "a ball" but made also to invoke an image of testicles. The idea was this: twin parties, one on each of two asteroids that were on a collision course with one another. Two DJs had been engaged and given similar instructions for their music selection but no specifics. They were also told nothing about the fact that the planets were on a collision course with one another. The monks, in their infinite wisdom, were recording both parties. The idea was that they would have both parties start three hours before collision. At the last minute, as all the guests were escaping in their various ways, the monks would whisk both DJs off to safety. The monks would then go back to their secret enclave and run both videos side by side to see exactly when what they were calling "The First Instance" would occur. By this, they meant when both DJs, independent of one another, would play the same song at the same time. This, they said, would be proof of…something or other. To be honest, I lose track of the whole thing. Impermanence and synchronicity and entanglement or something. I was mostly interested in the party because it would be, as my agent (so early in my career that I only had the one, you understand), "great exposure."

Within a few minutes of being there, I can honestly say I was bored. I don't know how to explain this properly, but when you spend enough time hanging out with extremely beautiful people doing wildly erotic things hyped up on fabulous chemicals that make you feel as if you're a young god, a party filled with relatively ordinary looking people is difficult to be excited about. Later, of course, this would be reversed— the novelty of people with imperfections would become, in itself, erotically charged. This was still early enough, though, that all I wanted was beautiful boys, five or six at a time.

So, like many young celebrities, I was sitting in the VIP lounge, drinking a ridiculously small batch and exclusive vodka ("label toward the front so any cameras passing by can passively read it, darling" my agent said) and scanning the room for anyone that could hold my interest.

"I hate these things," a voice from beside me said.

"Oh?" I asked without looking.

"Yeah. My agent says I had to come to this one, though. Said it would be good for the exposure." His voice was familiar enough that I knew if I looked I'd see someone from something I recognized. Still, I couldn't even be bothered.

"Same," I said and took a sip.

The DJs were in a identical booths built specifically so that they could hear the crowd, but no one could get close to them. The monks didn't want anyone whispering, "hey, did you know that there's another asteroid that's going to smack into this one in a few hours, and that there's a duplicate party going on over there?" to either of them. I had randomly wound up on the asteroid with the younger of the two male DJs, someone whose remixes I'd often heard on set as background music. I thought about trying to get close to him when the monks came to get him and then having him. I wondered what sort of music he'd like to play while we had sex.

I glanced over toward the door to see if anyone was arriving and that's when I saw the young man sitting next to me. Impossibly thin (something I was into at the time for some odd reason), two-tone hair as was the style at the time, and a cybernetically enhanced voice box. His eyes were enormous and continuously cycling through shades of blue that must have been outrageously expensive. The suit he was wearing would have cost him as much as many people pay for their homes. His boots were some sort of animal skin that I would bet was not synthetic. In other words, he was just hip enough to catch my attention.

"Do you want to fuck?" I asked. You have to understand that, in the life I had been living for the last few years, this was as causal a question as asking if someone would like a hit off your weedvape or if they needed a tissue after sneezing.

"Excuse me?" the boy asked, leaning in.

"I'm bored," I said. "Do you want to fuck?"

"Oh," he said and leaned back a bit. "Uh, sure. Where would you like to..." I'm sure he was about to ask me where I'd like to go in order for us to have some privacy, but privacy wasn't something I had even considered. Using my knee as a pivot, I slid around and onto his lap, and I removed his coat. His tongue tasted like raspberry candy and I noted that his breath was slightly cool from interacting with the metal of the voice box. His shirt was off and I'd already gotten his fly taken care of when I noticed a small crowd gathering nearby. He hadn't noticed yet.

There are a few different body types that humans tend to have, I've learned over time. A person can diet and exercise or use all kinds of surgery to try to change theirs, but overall the tendency is for about four types. The kind that men who are attracted to men tend to like is the one that is about six foot to six foot three or so, basically V shaped through the torso, with large feet and hands. There is a subset of that body type that is especially prized where the metabolism is so high that the male in question appears slightly starved—extremely small waist size, very small wrists and very large ankles despite large shoulder width. That particular body type tends to come with a penis that is larger than average. There's nothing wrong with having that body type or any other... it's a genetic thing and for the most part, unless one is obscenely rich, one cannot afford to do much about their genetics. However, considering the preference for this body type and the subtype especially, most filmed entertainment involves people who don't look like this watching people who *do* look like this in every film they consume. I point all this out because I myself am of the subtype and this young man, who I had placed as a relatively new-on-the-scene pop music star that had captured the imagination of the inner planets, was of the subtype as well.

The fact that two young men deemed "beautiful" by the narrow standards of the media culture, both having some degree of the public's attention, were together in one place would already have been enough for the photohounds to gather. The fact that they were now somewhere between foreplay, brief as it was, and full penetration on a couch in the VIP lounge in a public place meant that the story would be first in the entertainment segment on any of the news programs.

By that point, I had already gained a certain amount of detachment from such things, but I did note as I began riding him that his penis was enormous. Watching him, his head laid back on the couch, his eyes closed, his neck so open and vulnerable, even with the polished steel of the VOXBOX, I wondered what his other partners who were maybe not so versed in how to deal with something so large felt upon seeing it. For some reason, that train of thought, moreso than anything about him physically, got my motor running, so to speak. Thinking about a young man with such gentle tendencies having to hurt his partners simply to have sex with them, the unavoidableness of it, seeming almost like a betrayal in a sense, was far more erotic than even the fact that we were currently surrounded by a crowd of onlookers as well as a swarm of drones.

I'd already had my three shots this month, as anyone who works in the industry is required, so when his legs and face started twitching, I didn't stop him. I wanted to give the newsfeeds a show, so I touched his nipples, knowing that this would, if he was anything like almost all the other young men I'd been with, most likely set him off. I couldn't have predicted how much, though. His eyes flew open and he grabbed my hips, holding me in place with a strength I hadn't guessed he had, as his whole body seized upwards into me, even his toes flexing. The sound that came out of him was of such utter surprise that somewhere, in the back of my mind, I began to guess at what I would come to know later.

I thanked him and we kissed some more, then I got my clothes on and walked to where my shuttle was parked. It was only later, on the news feeds, that I saw him slowly try to put his clothes back on as he came to realize he had been watched through the whole thing. Almost immediately, his career was ruined. Not because he had any preference for males—his audience would have been just fine with that. No, they abandoned him for two reasons, both of which show the fickle nature of a public's love. Many abandoned him because they had only been paying attention wondering what he might look like naked, imagining what it would be like to see him in such an intimate way, to have sex with him, to know what sounds he made, etc. Once they say that, they no longer cared—their attention proven to last the space of exactly one orgasm. The rest abandoned him because he was now "used"—they had only wanted him because of his somewhat virginal nature. Their desire was to watch as he encountered things for the first time and to somehow relive their own innocence, if we can use that word, through him. To suddenly see him as a complex creature with a sexuality that was already developed in some way spoiled their fantasy of seeing him *slowly* be corrupted while they watched.

There were a small contingent who had actually followed him because they liked his music. They stuck around, of course, but it simply wasn't enough. The poor young man attempted to continue on with his career, but there was just no regaining that early spark. After a few more albums he retired from public life. I suppose I should have felt bad, but I truly didn't feel anything much about it. He tried writing me a few times; I never answered. It was in those letters that I found out

I had been his first. When someone says that you can never be sure if they are telling the truth or not, but I did think about what it must be like to have video of your very first time that you can go back to again and again if you choose.

I did feel somewhat bad, though, that something I had done simply so that I could get the media attention and then go home took so much of the focus that when the monks later released the news that they had found it, the evidence that there is synchronicity or whatever in the universe, all it did was ignite a second round of stories about that young pop music star wondering where he was now.

# SYLAS

The young man in the air mask has said nothing on the entire walk here. I am practically bouncing on my heels I am so proud of myself for getting the code. I am desperate to tell Sylas about it.

I poke my head through the hatchway. Sylas is standing near the windows, the deep blue nothing reflecting onto his face.

I immediately sense something is wrong.

I step up behind him.

"Sylas?" I ask.

He turns and sits down heavily. He doesn't look at me.

"What is it?" I ask.

He opens his hands as if about to explain something, then shakes his head and closes them into fists again.

"Disaster," he says.

I wait for him to explain but he says nothing.

"Has someone been caught? I haven't heard anything from Olver, so I don't think that..."

"The clone," Sylas says.

"Something has happened to the clone?" I ask.

He nods. "The maturation process was near completion. We were so close. *So close.*"

"Do you mean Salil? What happened?"

He sighs. "There was some...malfunction. I can't begin to trace it.

They are looking over the data, now. As if that will help anything." He shakes his head again.

I grab his shoulders and turn him toward me. "Tell me what has happened."

"The clone is dead," he says, still not looking at me. "It was fine one minute and then some sort of...some sort of *catastrophic* failure occurred and within seconds it...it disintegrated. It opened its eyes and placed its hand against the side of the tank and then the tissue began to break down. So *quickly*. It dissolved. Vanished right before my eyes."

The boy had a name. Sylas is avoiding using it.

"Why are you being so cold?" I ask.

He says nothing. Finally, the silence is too heavy.

I let go of his shoulders and sit back. "Can...can you make another one?"

He shakes his head. "Maturation takes time. There is not enough time to create another one and mature it to the correct age and remain on schedule."

We sat in silence.

"Is...is there some way to do it without the clone? Disguises, maybe? Surgical alteration?"

"We thought of all that before we started down the path with the clone. The answer is yes, but it's far more chancy. In all the simulations, the surgically altered thumb print or retina didn't pass security scans seventy percent of the time," Sylas says.

"Yes, but there's no choice at this point," I say.

"There is. One path. One I desperately hoped we could avoid, my love," he says and then looks at me. "You will have to kill him."

I should be shocked or upset, but what it feels like in that moment is perfect. Like a bending line suddenly connecting to make a circle. As if it was always going to turn out this way. As if turning out this way was exactly what the universe demanded.

"Yes," I say.

# THE PAST

"So this," the man said as he brought out a large tray filled with equipment, "will record all of those chemical reactions."

I pulled my robe a bit tighter around me.

"My…my smells?" I asked.

"Yes," the man said, then patted the bed. "As you know, we've tried various forms of this technology before to…hmm…assorted effects. This is the absolute latest in the technology, though. With this, we will be able to record the chemical interactions your body goes through as you reach climax and then relax afterwards. Once we have that data, we will be able to manipulate it in whatever way we wish to provide the customer with the ultimate in sensory experience."

I had heard this same pitch many times already. At the theaters equipped to give them the full sensory experience, most people just reported being able to smell vague hints of something decaying nearby. I didn't have a lot of hope about the new technology.

"So I'll just get on the bed and then…?" I asked.

"If you like. However, if you would prefer, we also have these," the man said and brought over another tray. On it I recognized different pieces of equipment designed to get at different difficult to reach places and to stimulate them in various combinations.

Some of them mirrors of things I had at home.

"Ah," I said.

He patted the bed again and smiled.

"Will you be here?" I asked.

"Yes," he said. "However, I will be monitoring from a safe distance. After all, we don't want my chemical reactions to be recorded." He laughed a cute, small laugh. "Customers aren't paying to be able to smell *me*, after all."

I walked to the bed, took my robe off, and got on. The plastic was cold. Before I could say anything about it, though, I heard a click. When I looked over he was already at a console near the far wall. "The heated pads should be coming on now."

The tray with all the equipment I'd never seen before came to life with an ominous low hum, a collection of small screens glowing amber or blue, giving readouts that I didn't understand. "...and we're live," he said. "You can start when you like."

The small wave of weirdness passed quickly as I reminded myself that this was only the first time I would pleasure myself today, and likely not even the first time there would be someone else in the room while I did it.

I reached for the devices that I was familiar with. I pictured the young tech coming over and shyly touching me. I pictured him getting more and more bold, eventually taking control of my movement. I pictured him eventually losing all of his inhibition and taking his lab coat off, then the rest of his clothes. I pictured him as one of those who is all shy and quiet, all glasses and button up shirts, but when the clothes come off, they are extremely well endowed. I pictured him sliding in to me and releasing long pent up and powerful feeling that he had to stifle every day because of his job. I pictured him whispering terrible, awful things into my ear. I pictured myself saying "but what about the measurements?" and him responding that he didn't care, that I had simply tempted him to the point he couldn't control himself. I pictured him pounding away at me to a point that I was not sure if what I was experiencing was pain or pleasure. I said to him that I was about to and before I could finish saying it, I pictured him putting his hand over my mouth and exploding inside me as I exploded all over myself. I pictured watching him slowly come back to himself, his animal side sliding back behind its covers as his front brain took over from his lizard brain once more.

When I opened my eyes, he was still all the way across the room.

"Excellent," he said. "I think we got some fantastic readings on that one."

The equipment on the tray next to me stopped humming, its little screens going dark.

"There are tissues right next to you," he said. "You can leave the other…instruments. Someone will be along to take those to sterilization."

I cleaned myself up.

"Someone will be along shortly to take you back to your clothes. Have a nice day," he said.

For a moment I wondered how he could be so cold after what we had just shared. Then I remembered, and put my robe back on.

They attached the new technology to a film that was fairly popular I had done a year ago and re-released it.

The critics said it truly did smell wonderful.

# OLVER

"The general said that you had shown some skill at piloting the armored suit, my love," Olver's voice says in my right ear, "but I must admit that I had thought perhaps he was telling me something because he knew it would please me. I am very happy to see that he was not. Your command of the controls is very good."

We're both standing on one of the main streets in one of the residential pods. Around us, the streets are filled with his guards and the few residents who were curious enough to stay. Everyone else has disappeared. Sylas' voice is in my head saying that he's sure they all left because they couldn't be sure this wasn't some kind of policing action.

"Thank you," I say, "but it isn't quite that easy."

Olver laughs and I melt a little. His laugh is wonderful. When he's like this, I can almost forget Sylas, the plan, everything.

"Come, over this way is the new garden site we have planned," Olver says. I turn to look, marveling yet again at how the walls of the cockpit of the mech have disappeared. From my perspective, I'm simply in a chair floating twenty feet up. Olver moves his mech along a side street and I follow.

We come to a place where the yellow barrier tape surrounds a lot the same size as the rest of the buildings. Walkways defined by open planters crisscross the area. The soil looks rich and black. The sensors tell me that it is full of nutrients and water.

"We have a plan to put these in all across each level to create more green space. There were studies done that tell us that people do better, mentally, when they can see green spaces on their daily walks," Olver says. I can tell he's extremely proud.

"How long until they sprout?" I ask.

"Not long, now," Olver responds. "Some of the first ones that were made down on the lowest levels have already begun to bud, in fact. The people love them. I can show you those tomorrow."

"Perhaps without the mechs," I say.

Again, Olver laughs.

"Perhaps," he says. His mech begins moving again and I make mine follow.

He's not wrong; the controls have tuned in to my mind, somehow, and I am both the giant and the thing riding in the belly of the giant. It is the trick of this doubled consciousness that makes the whole act of moving the mech both difficult and ridiculously easy.

I look again at the set of controls to my right that Olver has forbidden me from touching. Those are the weapons, he said, and they are only to be used in absolute last resort when in the spaces where people live. This makes me think of Sylas. I think of what just one of these tin soldiers could do to his group. To him. I shudder.

"Keep up, beloved," Olver says. I see that he's gone quite far from me. I move to catch up.

We round another street and move to the edge of what has been made to look like an undeveloped forested area. The illusion is quite convincing, up to and including a ragged boundary rather than a perfectly aligned one.

"Here, too, the project continues," Olver says. "I have made it mandatory for them to leave some spaces undeveloped unless it becomes a dire emergency. I believe with some proper guidance and motivation, people can keep the population down. We can have enough room for everyone without sacrificing space. The studies show that when any living area outgrows its green spaces, stress on that population increases tenfold. Violence and tribalism set in," he says. I hear in his voice itself how much he cares. For the millionth time, I wonder what might happen if only Olver and Sylas could sit down, work through their concerns together.

As if on a cue, a signal comes through. "Your highness, signal 138. Repeat, signal 138."

I can see the faces of the guard patrol who are not in mechs grow concerned. Weapons are unholstered. The sensors tell me that the three guards who are currently in my field of vision just flicked the safeties off on their small machine guns.

"What does that mean?" I ask.

"It is nothing, my love. Come, over here you can see..."

"Your Highness, signal 139. Repeat, 139," a different voice says.

"Location?" I hear him say. I can tell he's rattled. Not just in his voice, but that he hasn't tried to keep any of this from me.

"Two blocks to the East. Recommend crash."

There is silence. I hear him breathe deeply.

"What's going on?" I ask.

"I concur. Ground units, signal 2. Repeat, signal 2." The second Olver says this, the controls around me go from being clear white light behind them to yellow. I know from the many times I've seen this that it means someone else, almost certainly Olver, is now controlling the mech by remote. "I'm sorry, my beloved, but it seems our outing is over for the day."

About two blocks to the East I can see smoke rising. Olver moves both of our mechs back along the route we had just come from. I can see that many of our guards have moved away. Those that are left are jogging to keep up with us. With the controls no longer reporting to me, I have no sense of how fast we are moving. All I can do is sit cocooned in metal and wait until I'm told something.

We very quickly make it back to the access tunnel that we used to get from the hangar to this part of the station. The huge door closes behind us and the lights in the tunnel come on. Olver is walking us both back in the direction of the hangar.

"What happened?" I ask, hoping that he'll talk to me now that we are in safety.

"Once we are back to the palace," Olver says. The tension in his voice has ramped up rather than gone down.

Once we're back in the hangar, he parks our mecha. The walls of the cockpit go dark. The fluid drains; I cough up the last bit of it. The hatch opens. I unfasten the harness and move out onto the lip of the cockpit. Olver is already out of his suit and down the ladder. He gestures for me to follow and I do.

Once I'm down and my helmet is off he pulls me close and holds me. Around us, guards stand ready. They thoroughly search the three techs who come up to us. Once they are cleared, the young men take our helmets and we strip out of our pilot jumpsuits, handing them over as well. We're then hurried to a waiting pod.

Olver says nothing during this time, occasionally putting his hand up to his ear. He is still receiving signals, information about what's going on outside.

Once the pod stops and the doors open, we emerge back into the palace. He gives a few short orders to the staff and I stop.

"Tell me what is happening. Now," I say.

He sighs, dismissing the staff with a gesture.

"There was an explosion along the route we were to take next. When the men examined the site, they found that there were…people there…people who then fired weapons at them. They had to deal with this." I can see for just a second that Olver is tired. His shoulders sag a bit. "Since we have left the area, they have captured one of them. They are currently getting information from him."

"Was the…?" I begin but don't know what to say next. I have to be careful not to reveal what I know. This is just like before. Again, I wonder, who is it? Do I know them? What do they know about me? Is a face I know already revealing everything about me to one of Olver's men as I stand here in the royal palace?

"The explosion meant for us? The men think it is likely, considering that it happened along the exact route we were to have gone. Had I not detoured us to see the unused space, we would likely have been at that exact area when the device was detonated," Olver says. "Do not worry, though, beloved. We will find out who did this. We will root out their group and make them pay for it." He smiles. This is all meant to comfort me.

He doesn't know what I know.

# THE PAST

I spent a lot of my high school years in other boys' beds.

I'm not proud of it, nor am I ashamed of it. It is simply what happened.

To be honest, if I could have skipped the school part, I would have. They enforce attendance, though. They want to make sure that you get a belly full of their ideology.

One of my most fond memories was of the three young men on our Lacrosse team. It's funny how, no matter how technologically advanced we get, our ideas of how to spend time never seem to change—chasing a ball around, testing luck with cards or dice, etc. I didn't play the sport, of course. Joining into things like that has never made sense to me. Clubs or sports or religions…joining things…puts you at the mercy of other people's whims and that gives them power over you. At that age I could never have put together the words for that, but it was already a strong feeling I had.

One of the young men on the team had caught my eye because we shared several classes my first year in high school. I won't bore you with the cycle of flirtations, testing, teasing, etc. You know how boys are with one another at that age. It's all "give me attention" but then taunts of "are you giving me attention?" Eventually I was invited to a party at the nearby lake.

When I arrived, he was alone. Very quickly we began to do the things that teenagers tend to do when they can find a moment alone together, which was nice after so long a period of anticipation. Some part of me felt a bit like a predator considering how many sexual partners I'd already had versus how few it very quickly became evident he'd had. Still, it was a nice evening—shy is still, to this day, one of my favorite flavors of person. We made plans to meet again the following weekend.

The next weekend I arrived as I had before. He was alone as he had been. Very soon after that, though, two other boys arrived. They were also from the team. He explained that they were already a couple, and that they wanted to join us in our sex that evening. What I remember was having to try to control my laughter as he spent twenty minutes trying to convince me, thinking I would reject this idea. As you can imagine, I said yes.

What I was unprepared for, though, was the feelings that this created in for me. This was my first time having sex with more than one partner at a time. I'd been to parties with older men where a number of them were going to have sex with me, but that had always been one at a time. There was a different energy to this, and it was powerful—all of us young, all of us naked underneath the moon beside the lake, together.

For a time, I stopped making time for anyone else. This caused some financial difficulties, as you might imagine, but the connection was something new to me. As I said, I did not join things, but this connection was formidable. After a few more times, there were dates where all four of us would be together for plays or movies or dinners. I came to know all of them as individuals; their fears, their hopes, the special ways each wanted to be loved that were different, sometimes only in tiny ways, from one another.

We were one thing.

Of course, as it always must, such a beautiful time came to an end.

One of them found out about what my life was like before they came into it. What's funny is that I can't remember how...some jealous betrayal by one of the young women who were constantly floating into and out of my life, perhaps, letting slip the information to get revenge for not being able to have one of the young men she yearned in vain for. Maybe, or I may have made that up. Regardless, once they discovered the "kind of person" I was, as one of them said, they considered it a violation of their trust that I hadn't come forward with the information already. At the time I was too hurt to say anything, but all these years later my only thought is that I should have asked them if their reaction would have been any different had I told them versus however they had found out. We all know it wouldn't have been. Either way, I would have been ejected.

You see, in their minds, what made the connection was that we were all young and experiencing the novelty of this grouping on the same level. Young minds tend to deal in absolutes. There was no room in their way of seeing what we all had for the idea that even with all of my experiences, this was still unique and precious.

I was immediately shunned. Of course, I was not without sex for very long. I never have been. But it took a long time for the majority of the hurt to stop.

Through the web of rumor I heard about their various breakups and trists over the years. They meant less and less to me given time. When I come across pictures of them through various media, this one grown fat with a beard, this one posing with his many children, this one in his uniform, I only see in them the freckled thin-shouldered boys that they were.

As you can see, the damage never totally healed.

# SYLAS

I slide down off of Sylas' hips and we lay next to each other panting.

I look over at his lean, powerful body and feel pride that I can make such a strong man so weak.

He reaches beside us and pulls the small canteen he always has with him to his lips. He offers it to me once he's done. Nothing in the world has ever tasted so good as the cold, flat, metallic water from that beat up canteen.

I hand it back to him. When I've caught my breath, I ask, "So which do you love?"

"Are you asking me to choose between your mind and your body?" Sylas asks.

"Yes," I say, running my hand down his chest.

"It is an impossible task. You ask me to think in terms of a split when there is none. You are you, and this includes all aspects."

"Bull," I say. "You might like all things about me, though I don't buy that at all, but there is one part you love more than the others. It's simply how people work."

"Not me," Sylas says. "When I was younger, I had relationships like that. I think that is essentially a young man's way of being, though—to chop things up into their component parts and declare love for one over the other. It is a mistake of the inexperienced."

"So you're trying to tell me that you love everything about me?" I ask.

"If I did not, it would not be you that I loved, but parts of you, or some echo of you that existed only in my mind. Don't confuse me with one of the men who want the you that appears in your videos. I want the real you."

"Even after we…finish…the thing?" I ask looking up at him.

He pulls me closer. "*Especially* then. You will be a hero to all of us, but I won't love your hero self any less or more than any other part of you."

"I like the sound of that," I say.

"…but you don't believe it. I understand this. It will take time before you see. It is a good thing that I am patient," Sylas says, then kisses me. "The plan now has a certain simplicity to it that belies the work of forces beyond our knowing." He raises both hands. "My men and I storm the launch bay and with the codes you have brought us we take the mechs and use them to bring order to the streets," he says with a slight shake of his left hand. Then with the same gesture on his right he says, "and at the same time, you take Olver's gun from his hip and shoot him. In the control room there won't be more than two other people. They will be in such shock that you will have an easy time dispatching them with his gun as well."

The quiet stretches between us.

"The new government won't be a deception this way. If I am honest, I was never completely comfortable with that idea to begin with. In this, it will be our faces that the people see. They will know us, love us, trust us."

"But what if I can't…what if I can't pull the trigger?"

He pauses. "You must. And it is because you must that it will happen."

218

I stare into his eyes.

He sees how confused I am. "Don't you see? The failure of the clone plan means that you were always going to be the one to pull the trigger. It was always going to be you because the universe does not waste anything."

"It was always going to be you," he says once more, and I lose myself in his lips, his hands, his hips again.

# LIKE SOMETHING FROM A DREAM

Day 45 of what "Coach" calls my new life.

Today I learn weapons.

Today I learn the gun.

There will be many models of it.

Many different kinds.

This one in my hand, whatever they call it, is always "the gun."

It has moods "Coach" tells me.

Some days it is shy and must be coaxed.

Some days it is vengeful and must be brought to heel.

It is louder than I am.

Its voice always decides the future.

We can pretend that the voices of poets, of singers, of politicians are powerful.

But the gun? It knows better.

I am the only one in the universe that can bring this gun to bear.

It is mine as I am its.

We exist as one thing.

No arm.

No hand.

No finger.

No trigger.

No barrel.

No bullet.

One thing.

My heart to theirs—a direct line connecting death's whisper to their ear.

I learn the gun. This particular one is called a pistol.

I learn 3 yards. Then 5. Then 7. Then 10.

I learn the gun. This particular one is called the rifle.

I learn 3 yards. Then 5. Then 7. Then 10. Then 20. Then 50. Then 100.

"Coach" says that's good.

He says we could do more. Go further. But that's not the point.

The point of you, "Coach" says, is to be close. To be right up under the target before they even know they're in danger.

I learn that I am not medals.

I will never be given a parade.

What I do is ugly. Horrible.

But necessary.

What I do is quiet.

What I do is shadow.

So I learn other things. Like how to smile. "Coach" says that can be just as deadly a weapon as a gun.

I learn how to listen to what is really being said.

The difference between a yes that means no and a yes that means yes.

I learn to do things with my body.

That people will tell you more when they are relaxing after sex than a violent and bloody interrogation could ever reveal.

I learn how to sigh. Which fork to use at what time during a dinner.

I learn weapons.
There are many different kinds.

# THE PAST

I would come to find out that it takes about three weeks to feel normal again after any period of time in hypersleep. "The freezer, darling," my friend Kinsley said as we sipped drinks at our favorite bar what had seemed to me just a few short months ago.

As I came out of the pod that first time, though, it seemed to me as if I would never feel well again. It isn't terribly sexy what happens to the body the first 24 hours after being woken up, that's for sure. Especially back then, so early in the cycle of technology. These days, they just drug you through it all. You come out and then spend then next day or so going in and out of the condition. Designer stuff that the companies make themselves, marked on the package as "gentle transition" or "languid wake." All of it designed to make you feel better about the fact that someone is making minimum wage to clean your various orifices while your body slowly regains control of itself after having been taken down to nearly 320 degrees below zero or so.

I know that sounds confusing, but I'll get to that.

Before I'd gone in, they'd warned me about all of that. The company had assured me there would be people on both sides ready to take care of me and pamper me back to wakefulness. It was all included in the price. That would not always be the case, but I'll get to that later, too.

They'd also warned me about time dilation. Back then, we weren't even going all that fast. The transport I was to leave on was the latest from the company that I won't name because they'd long since gone out of fashion, then existence. Still, at the time, this was the name that was in all the glossiest of hardcopy magazine ads. They had all the hottest and sexiest young stars in tight white underwear yawning, then smiling as they stretched, as if they'd just woken up on a Sunday afternoon from a nap. This transport was the fastest ship ever built at the time, the pride of the company. We would eventually reach "a cruising speed of 10% of the speed of light!," they assured me. I could hear the exclamation mark every time they said it.

At the time, it excited me, too.

Eventually, I'd come to recognize that this was merely part of the pitch. I'd go through a lot of these companies and a lot of their excitement about the new speed their latest cruiser was able to achieve. Invariably, once things had ended and I was on my way back to wherever I was calling home at the time, I would see that same proud cruiser now serving the discount fliers as I boarded the new "latest cruiser," now traveling at 14% of the speed of light! (the exclamation point still heard, but perhaps less impactful on me than before).

What they warned me about was that problematic issue of physics. The closer one gets to the speed of light, the slower time moves. They call it time dilation or special relativity, I'm told. I would love to explain it to you more, but I swear that the more times it's been explained to me, the less I understand it. Something about clocks and sea level and... it's all maddening when someone tries to tell it to me. The end result, though, is that if one leaves a planet and accelerates to what sounds relatively slow ("10% of the speed of light" is likely to garner the response "is that all?" from someone, like myself, who knows so little) but is actually blindingly fast, time moves differently for them than anyone that person has left behind on said planet. The result is that for the person traveling away from the planet, time moves slower. Once that traveler reaches where they are going, perhaps only 6 years have passed whereas for the person left behind on the planet, 10 years may have passed. The faster one goes, the greater the differences between time's passage, if you see what the whole thing is getting at.

At least, again, that's what they told me.

It all seemed a bit farcical, if I'm honest. As if they were having me on.

The effects of it are very real, though.

The first few times were incredibly jarring even though I had been warned what to expect.

The transport service on my first trip not only took care of me through the twilight while my throat and bowels learned to work on their own again, they transported me to their private facility back planetside. I woke up in a lovely soft bed covered by a just-heavy-enough duvet in a room bathed in gentle midmorning sunlight that smelled of fresh cut lavender. A chime and a voice announced that it had just turned eleven-thirty. I awoke, showered, got dressed in the clothes I'd left behind for them to set aside for me upon awakening and walked through the door into a very pleasant hallway.

You see, they were aware of how jarring the shift was going to be for passengers, and so they designed their waking facility to have almost no technology. No markers of how much things may have changed. No matter when one woke up in the facility, they would see no evidence that anything had changed at all while they were away. Again, one of the many premium services they set aside for their "guests."

A young woman met me and we confirmed that all of the details I'd asked for had been taken care of. The last detail on their checklist was waiting for me outside; a car carrying my luggage would take me to the condo I owned at the time. I thanked her and retrieved the small bag I'd left with them that contained my keys, my sunglasses, and my telephone. I put on the sunglasses I had an affect of wearing at the time, and then left the facility.

The changes I saw once I was outside were immediately unnerving, though. Architecture had gone through a revolution while I was away, it seemed. Buildings were now being made to move and sway with the wind. The first time I saw a fifty-story building lean from one side to the other in a stiff breeze brought my heart to a stop. While I was away, they had apparently also advanced enough to make hovering cars. The vehicle that picked me up was a conversion—a very old model of large black car that had been converted to hover. I got in and tried to pretend I wasn't unsettled to find the autonomous limousine lifting itself thirty feet above the road and then gliding through the streets with silent assurance as if it had always existed.

My building hadn't been converted to the new style, though, and so it was a relief to find it there, still plain glass and steel as before. The limo thanked me as I closed the door and took my bag into the lobby. The doorman was disturbingly young, but knew my name and welcomed me home. He informed me that someone from the company had already been by that day (as they had been every week, another premium service for their "guests" that I had paid for in advance) to take my mail in. I thanked him.

The elevator had no buttons. I was in a mild panic until another resident got in and simply spoke his floor out loud. He and I exchanged a smile, but I didn't recognize him at all. Once he got out and the doors closed, I spoke my floor. The lift whooshed to the top floor.

I finally exhaled to find my place exactly as I had left it. The person who had been paid to come in had left all my mail on the kitchen table as they had been instructed, and had kept the place dusted and straightened. The pile of mail was enormous, though. Boxes and envelopes and a few metal tubes. I couldn't handle the thought of diving into it. Instead, I poured myself a scotch and dialed Thomas on my phone.

And almost dropped the glass when an old man answered.

"I'm sorry, I—," I started to say.

"There you are, darling," Thomas' voice came back. More rasp to it, but unmistakable. It was attached to an old man, though. Hair receding, crows feet, almost completely steel gray covering his head. "I was wondering if you were going to wake up today."

"Thomas," I said, careful not to put the question mark at the end.

"Well, of course it is, darling. Who else? Look, it's obvious you've only just decanted. I'll come by and we'll have drinks." The screen went blank.

He did come by that night. He came in walking with a cane. "They want me to just go on and get the surgery, don't you know, but I am not interested. I like the cane. It's a nice prop, isn't it? Gives one distinction and all that." It took many drinks before I could reconcile this old man with the devilish grin of the peer I'd left behind. He was kind about it. "I suppose I must look an absolute fright, darling. One can't blame you. From your perspective you've only been gone…what…two years or so?" he laughed at something, but as he looked away I could see tears in his eyes. "With your travel time included, you've been away for almost ten years." On some level, I had known that, but it still hit me as a shock. "Oh, come now, there's no need to pull such a face. This is how we knew this thing would work, didn't we?"

We spent the rest of the night catching up until his husband of the last three years called and told him to come home. Once he was gone, I was left with nothing but my empty condo. I contacted a service and

227

had them send over an obscenely young looking blonde. He spoke in a slang that I almost couldn't understand. I told him to keep his stupid mouth shut and then I did unspeakable things to him until I was tired enough to go back to sleep. Over the next few months I got back in touch with my agency only to find my agent had aged in the same fashion. Again, I should have been able to expect it, but it also came as a shock. I told him to book me a few films. He reminded me that with all I'd invested when I left, I never needed to do films again. I told him I wanted to, though, so he booked a few.

The second contract trip offer came in and I took it. It was for about the same time terms. I won't get into details about who he was, but you've used his company's products. When I arrived back planetside, both my agent and Thomas were dead. The agent had passed me off to a younger man who thanked me profusely—having my account made him someone of major importance at his office. Thomas' husband, now the same age Thomas had been when I came home the first time (he always did like them younger) sent over a message that had been recorded for me.

The old man who appeared on the screen looked almost nothing like Thomas. The only part that was still him was around the eyes when he smiled. "Ah, there you are, old boy," he said. The rasp and wheeze of his voice instantly made me cry. "Now, look, there's no need for all that rot. Stiff upper lip and so on. I've had a good life. I suspect you have, too. This is, of course, the part where I'm supposed to tell you some life lesson I've learned and then you rethink your whole life and have a happy existence. Well, I've always thought that was horseshit of the worst order. You've discovered the fountain of youth! Why would I ever say anything other than congratulations! They're saying that the latest science now that they have so much data from travelers is that the time

228

dilation is even greater than we thought, and that the effects are quite lasting." At this, he laughed then sighed. "It seems you are a man come unstuck from time, my dear. And I salute you for it." At this he devolved into a coughing fit that grew worse and worse and then the recording snapped off. A few days later I could finally bring myself to look at the difference between the "recorded on" date of the video and his death date. They were only 24 hours apart.

Another contract offer was already waiting for me to decide on. I took it immediately, contacted my agent, left instructions for him to sell the condo and invest an even greater percentage of the money that was in the account, and I left the next day.

# OLVER

"Still, I hope that all of this unrest hasn't turned you away from the idea of our jaunts, my love," Olver says.

I finish zipping up my jumpsuit. We're taking the mechs out again.

Olver finishes zipping up his own suit. The soldiers nearby are all on alert. Having him so close by makes them nervous.

At some point, Sylas repeats in my head, he'll want to take you out again. Get word to us. We'll handle the rest, he said.

I told them today.

As soon as Olver told me that today was the day he wanted to go again, I knew that meant today was when it would happen. I glance at the chronometer on the wristband of the suit. By now, they should be gathered just outside those doors.

I just have to get him away from his guards.

"You seem distracted today, beloved," Olver says. He has stopped at the bottom of the lift near the foot of his mech. "We can put this off for another day if you don't feel well," he says.

"No," I say, perhaps too quick. "No, it's alright. I'm looking forward to this." That makes him smile.

"Open the hangar doors," he calls out to no one in particular. One of the perks of being in command—people will listen for orders, and so one doesn't have to be specific.

He turns and puts his hands on the rails of the lift.

Already I can hear the sounds of gunfire.

Already I can hear the sounds of men yelling.

It is happening now.

"Quickly, get his highness to the control room!" someone yells.

I turn to see Sylas' men flooding through the halfway open hangar doors. The firefight is fierce. I see a young man gunned down and I think, he had a mother. A father. He had hopes. Things he wanted for his life. All those things are over, now.

The bodyguards have grabbed Olver and are physically moving him away. He's yelling something and two of the guards grab me.

They will take you with them, Sylas' voice from before says. I remember his eyes as he leaned in closer to me. When they do, make sure that you still have your gun on you. It is essential for the plan to work that they get him to a place where he feels safe enough to not have armor on, for the guards to be distracted enough for you to get close. We're counting on you, Sylas had said, and then he kissed me.

In that moment, I knew that I'd do anything for him. If there had been any doubt, it was gone.

Just as Sylas predicted, they move us along a short corridor, closing heavy blast doors along the way. They get us into a room and close another heavy door behind us. The walls come to life with view screens and controls. On each screen, a scene of chaos and death. Sylas' men have found cover behind some of the mechs while the few men here in the hangar who had weapons are pinned down behind a few control panels. For now, there is a stand off, but even I can see it won't last long.

"How did they get in?" Olver asks. I hear his heartbreak. "How could they have known that now would be the time?"

He turns to look at me. I shake my head and feign upset. My acting skills aren't as needed as I thought they might be when Sylas and I were discussing this, Olver is so distracted. I genuinely feel terrible about all of this.

"They're breaking through the first blast door," one of the four guards who has made it into this room with us says.

On the screens, some of Olver's men have gotten control of a mech. They are using it to attack Sylas' men.

"You and you, find us a route out of here," Olver says, pointing at two of them. I can see that they don't want to go, but they leave through another doorway. "You and you, go and hold them off," he says. The remaining two leave back the way we came.

We are alone. His back is to me as he watches the screens.

The time is now.

You'll know when it happens, Sylas had said. It will be as clear as day to you, his voice whispered to me as he kissed me again.

It's been leading to this.

This moment.

I look again at the gun on Olver's belt. It still has the strap of leather buttoned across its handle. Because I knew that today was to be the day, the one I have does not.

I could pull it at any time.

It would take nothing, the merest gesture from my hand.

On the screens, I see the men, the ones Sylas told me about, the dedicated soldiers of peace, the ones who believe that they can and will bring justice to Olver for his crimes. They are being killed wholesale. Slaughtered. Cut down as though nothing more than tall grass.

Sylas may be among them.

I begin to shake.

I know that I must stop this.

I know that I must pull the gun from its holster.

I must put it to Olver's head.

I must pull the trigger.

I must.

I *must*.

On the screen, the gunshots grow further and further between.

The one mech that had been moving has stopped. I can see the young man hanging half in and half out of the cockpit.

Now.

It must be now.

So many have died trying to get us to this moment.

So many disappeared.

So much lost.

The shaking gets very bad.

Olver turns to me, puts his arm around me. "I know, my beloved. I know. It is hard to watch. Please do not think that I am unmoved. These young people, they were led to this by someone, surely. They turned from God and found themselves at the mercy of The Devil. Even as they die, it is my hope that they will find salvation of some kind in their afterlife." He presses me to him.

The gunshots are almost stopped.

It has to be now.

It *must* be now.

"Such a waste of lives," Olver says.

A nearby panel beeps. On the screen, one of the men leans into frame. "Units A and B report that they have the launch bay secure."

"You may speak in front of him," Olver says.

"Commander of unit B says he has a man in custody that they believe was the leader," the young man says.

I stop breathing.

Now.

*Now!*

"It's...My lord, it's Sylas."

I have to struggle to hide my physical reaction at hearing the name. Why did he come himself? Why not wait safely to see the outcome?

"Bring him to me," Olver says. The ice in his voice should steel my nerves, but it doesn't.

Another beep. The young man leans into frame once more. I know what he's going to say before he even says it.

"Commander unit B reporting that as they were securing Sylas, he took some sort of pill from a false tooth. They attempted to resuscitate, but it did not work," the young man says. "Sylas is dead."

This should be the moment. This should be the moment where I pull the gun from Olver's hip and put a hole in his head. I can see myself do it as I've seen myself do it so many times.

But I don't.

The two young men who left to find a secure route out come back in. They wait for instructions.

Olver exhales heavily. He nods as if something he has long known is confirmed. "A waste," he whispers. "Such a waste."

And it is in that moment that I know for certain that I won't kill Olver.

"Excuse me," I say, turn, and walk past the two men out of the room.


"Gentlemen," Olver says, standing. He holds out his champagne glass to the rest of the men gathered around the table. They all wear the smiles of self-congratulation and rest at ease. "It is with the greatest pleasure that I salute you in your victory over the rebels who tried to take our democracy from us," he says. The table erupts in good natured

234

laughter and applause.

The largest dining room has been decked out with the grandest place settings and serving dishes that the palace owns. Every single servant that I have ever seen in my time here now stands at the edges of this room ready to bring whatever Olver's slightest whim demands at a moment's notice. On the table already, only one course in, is enough food to provide for every starving face I have seen on this station. The men here mostly ignore it, treating what those below would consider a godsent gift as if it were merely decoration.

"We have routed the rebellion and brought its leaders to their knees," Olver says. Again, more laughter and applause. "Sylas, the malcontent who once had the audacity to sit at this very table, to call himself one of my most trusted, has been taken into custody." At the mention of his name, I have to look away. Around the table there is the hint of booing and hissing, as if this were some melodrama playing out on a stage. "Those who have helped him are being found even as we dine, here, and they, too, will face justice."

With that, the doors at the rear of the room open and in march five heavily armored and armed guards. My heart leaps into my throat.

They march further and further up the table.

They are coming for me, I know it.

I look around for any way out. I couldn't make it to any of the doors before they were on me. Would the few servants that I recognize from among Sylas' ranks even help me? I look down at the table. None of the knives that are here would be any good.

Could I kill myself before they take me?

I reach for the steak knife.

Before I can get my hand on it, though, the guards stop right behind one of the generals. Olver nods at them, his glass still extended.

The guards put their hand on the man's shoulder. He stops eating, gently putting his spoon back down into his soup. He wipes his mouth and puts his napkin next to his bowl, then stands.

He looks down the table at Olver, says something in a language I don't understand, then spits at him. One of the guards knocks the general on the back of the head with the butt of his rifle and then two others grab him under his arms. They drag him from the room. Within seconds, they are gone and the silence is deafening.

Olver raises his glass slightly more and smiles.

"To us!" Olver says.

"To us!" the table roars and they all down their glasses.

Olver sits and patches of conversation bloom around the table. He looks at me and smiles, putting his hand on my arm.

"What did you think of my speech?" he asks.

Before I can answer, one of the valets comes to my arm.

"Sir," the valet says.

"Yes?" I ask looking up from my plate for the first time in what feels like hours.

"Phone for you."

"Excuse me," I say, standing up and taking the phone. I walk to the edge of the room. On the screen is a face I recognize, but it takes me a minute to place her. Then it hits me: Aidy, the flight attendant from the ship that brought me here what seems like years ago.

I feel how hard my eyebrows furrow in confusion. "Yes?"

She smiles.

"Prince," she says, then the line goes dead.

# THE PAST

"No, you're not hearing me," my manager says.

"I am, but the idea is…" I say but have trouble putting my thought into words.

"Is what?"

"Is ridiculous. Why would someone need to…to…"

"Patent their own DNA? You're not paying attention," he says. "They are already at the point where they can bring your smells, your tastes, to your audience. What do you think is next?"

"What do *you* think is next?" I ask.

Thomas leans forward, "Last night I was talking with Jefferson Mintz about what his company is working on. It's…it's huge." He cocks his head a bit as if trying to decide something, then says, "Blanks."

"What does that mean?" I ask.

"Put a blank into a machine, select the person you most want to have sex with, and in the space of a few hours the machine produces that person."

"What?"

Thomas nods. "He says they're a few years off from it, but they already have the patent in the works."

"Cloning?"

"Even better," Thomas says. "From the second the blank becomes the person that's downloaded, they are already in the process of degrading. Do what you want with them for a few hours and then put them into another machine that receives the degraded genetic material. It's…it's genius, is what it is. The customer has to buy the printer, the degrading material collector, and a subscription to the service that has the imprints."

"It's disgusting."

"That's what everyone says about any advance in biological. What is the imprinted blank but a vibrator with a better motor, though?" Thomas says. His smile says he's already thinking about where he's going to put it in the house. "As my client, this is why I want you to patent your DNA…anyone who doesn't have theirs copyright protected will lose it automatically to this service because no one sees it coming."

"That's…"

"Yeah. Boo hoo. It's horrible. But it's happening. You can get out in front of it. Be the first to copyright your DNA patterns so that when the customers see that they can't have you, they start putting pressure on his service to get you and then they have to pay what we want to put your pattern into rotation."

"But the blanks…the imprints…aren't they…aren't they *me*?" I ask.

"In a sense. They have the same hips, the same cock, sure, all the physical parts that the customer wants, but that's what keeps bringing the customer back—they can get that close to you but they can't have your intelligence, your dreams. All the things that they truly want they can't have."

I thought about it for a moment. "And you say they are going ahead with this no matter what?" I ask.

He nods.

"Okay," I say. "Let's do it."

# EXTRACTION

I nearly fall over. I put my hand on the wall to brace myself. A flood of memories buries me for a moment and leaves me dizzy.

Where the fuck…?

Where am I?

I look around.

At the huge table behind me, guy at my six o'clock surrounded by his cronies looks a whole lot like Olver.

Ok, right, this must be the royal palace. If you can call a place like this on a shithole planet at the edge of fucking space "royal."

I feel for the gun in my jacket pocket, but it isn't there.

Okay. So phase one is over.

The Van Ryan cover worked, then.

"Are you alright, sir?" the valet says.

I stand up and straighten my jacket. I hand the phone back to him. I smooth back my hair. There is a mirror nearby. I move to it. The face looking back at me is Van Ryan, not mine. The face they told me to expect. I nod.

"Yeah, pal, I'm alright, thank you," I say. I put my hand on the guy's shoulder. "Actually, could you tell his highness I'm not feeling well and that I'm going back to my room?" The servant nods. I look over my shoulder one more time.

Time for phase two.

I find the nearest guy in a black suit with an earpiece.

"I need to get back to my room," I say. I don't know where the hell I'm going, and guys like this, they don't like having to babysit, but they prefer it if the important people they look after tell them where they're going, so the guy won't mind taking me. He fancies it, I'm guessing, more than having to run after me. I follow him without saying anything and if we don't happen to run in to anyone I'm supposed to talk to, this'll go smoothly.

Of course, though, it doesn't. We take the lift all the way up to one of the buttons that's unmarked. The guy had to put in his ID card to get us there, so I'm guessing this next stop will be the private quarters. As soon as the doors open, though, there's a tall goon waiting for us.

"Shall I draw a bath for you?" he asks. I stop myself from shaking my head. I'm sure Van Ryan loved the hell out of this bullshit.

"No, I can manage, there, pal," I say. There are a couple of doors, so I pause for a second. Right on schedule, the goon opens one of them just as the lift doors close. I step inside and the tall guy shuts the door behind me. I exhale and shed the dinner jacket immediately. I drop it on the stairs as I go down even though it looks expensive. I wish there was some way I could take it with me.

But there isn't.

I'm guessing I've got maybe an hour, tops, before Olver comes nosing around wanting his fucking dick sucked. I have to be a hundred percent ready for that moment because I'm not going to get another one. If I've been activated, it means the team is already descending from orbit. It won't be long before they begin the assault on the station. My cover would have thought they were all flight attendants and pilots from the ship that brought him here. He would have thought that they all left for

240

their next destination after dropping him off; just one in a long line of flights that crew was supposed to make.

"Coach" would be so proud, I think. For a second, I wonder if maybe the old bastard is still alive, somewhere. Maybe plugged into a machine or something. Unlikely, but who knows.

In reality, the crew have been hiding behind the nearest moon. A first-rate wetworks squad armed to the gills sitting on Olver's doorstep the whole time. I just have to take care of him.

First thing's first. I start opening cabinets and cupboards to find my luggage. I wish there'd been some way to tell Van Ryan not to let them hide the stuff, but anything I could have done would have risked him getting the idea of what we were doing. They said that any kind of contact could have caused some kind of psychic disturbance that could have lead to full on psychosis, and then the jig would be up.

Do I want to take a second to look at the stunning view out the huge window? Sure. Would I like to lounge around in this incredible room? You bet. In my head, though, there's a countdown running.

We're not going to get another shot at this.

Finally, I find where they've stored my luggage. I pull out the smallest case, the one where all the oils and ointments and whatever were stored. I unzip the lining and pull out the pistol that has been there since before I went into cold sleep back on Earth, kept safe from scans by all the chemicals in the so-called beauty products. It's so small there's barely room for my smallest finger on the handle. I slide it down the front of my boxers so it fits with only the slightest bulge. I also pull out the tiny comcard they gave me, and slide it right next to the gun.

Just in time, too, because upstairs I hear the door opening.

"My love?" someone calls out.

"Showtime," I whisper.

241

I manage to slide out of everything but the ridiculous neon-colored briefs Van Ryan had on and get under the covers of the enormous bed just before Olver comes through the door. He stops and cocks his head to the side and says, "they tell me you aren't feeling well." Smug piece of shit—his tone is the same one you'd take with a child. It's not easy to stay calm, but I just need him to get under the covers so the sound is muffled enough.

I think back to all the women I've been with. The ways they moved to get me to come to them. I mimic the movements and he crosses the room.

"Shall I ring for the doctor?" he asks. He stops at the edge of the bed.

"No," I whimper. "Come be with me," I say. I even reach out a bit to him.

"There are a few things that I need to…" he says.

I reach out a bit more and try to get the cover to fall away from my shoulder a bit. I know I could never resist a bare shoulder. I'm hoping he's the same.

"Well," he says, "perhaps a little bit of time won't hurt." He toes out of his shoes and pulls the covers back. He slides in and puts his arm under me. Look, it's not the first time I've been cuddled by a man, and it's never super pleasant, but the contact is kind of nice. To make sure he doesn't go anywhere, I pull myself in close. He closes the covers over us.

That's my cue.

"Now," he says, "what has you feeling so badly?" He finishes off by kissing my forehead. "I hope it wasn't the shellfish. You never said you had any…"

By this time I've gotten the pistol free and I have it against the side of his head.

"Don't. Fucking. Move," I say.

"Beloved? What is the meaning…?"

"Shut the fuck up," I say. Before he can do anything else, I snatch the covers up over his head and I press down on the side, making a little seal just behind the wrist of my other hand—it won't stop all of the splashback, but it will help. Then I pull the trigger. The covers snap out then settle. I pull the trigger again. The covers snap again then settle.

I slide backward out of the covers and off the bed. I'm splattered, but much less than I feared I would be. I won't lie, killing someone while buck naked? It gets me more than a little stiff.

You learn new things about yourself all the time, I guess.

The covers kept things from getting too messy, though, so think I can cover the blood up with clothes, which is good. I don't have much time to get from here to one of the airlocks and out. Not enough time to have to stop and clean myself at all. I set what has to be a speed record getting back into the suit from dinner.

Just then a small compartment in one of the walls opens up and a guy steps out carrying a gun. I hadn't planned on having to fight anyone, but I don't have a lot of choice at this point. I go into one of the stances "coach" taught me.

"I never would have thought you'd do it! Come; they're already on their way!" he says, gesturing back into the compartment.

I don't recognize the guy as one of the operatives, and I haven't given any of the code words yet, but who knows—maybe there were contingencies. "On their way?" I ask.

"Any powerful air discharge. They know that there are ways to disguise weapons and to hide weapons fire, so the sensors are keyed to the one thing that could still never be faked from a weapon—an intense localized push of air pressure. It's the one level of security we could never defeat without setting it off. Now, come!" He grabs for my wrist. Two things are apparent: one, he knows Van Ryan, and two, he's not upset about Van Ryan killing Olver. Whoever the guy is, I'm thinking I can take advantage of these things to get to an airlock. I take a chance and let him drag me.

●

The guy keeps babbling on about the revolution and some kind of plan. He's talking and talking and talking. It dawns on me this guy must've had a thing for Van Ryan.

"I apologize for the necessity for making you believe I had been killed, my love. It was one of our tactics in case of a massive defeat," the guy says. I don't say anything, as I'm too busy trying to figure out which nodes and junctions we're passing. I'm also running back through the list of major players that they gave me, but this guy doesn't seem familiar. Surely the team is here, by now. I just have to find them. "A nasty bit of face transforming technology that we paid a great deal of money for. By the time the autopsy was underway, the effect would have worn off, of course."

We run across a couple of goons with rifles. Typical downtrodden freedom fighter types. They're handing me a jumpsuit to climb into and some boots to squeeze on. One hands me a pistol. One calls the guy dragging me Sylas, and then it all clicks. Of course—the security guy that was Olver's boyfriend at one time. That makes sense, then. Afterwards he must've started a resistance. That must be these guys.

How did Van Ryan get himself mixed up with this lot?

Sylas drags me through some more corridors until I can tell we're

244

getting close to an airlock. I'm about to put one in the back of the guy's head when we come under fire. We duck back around the corner. They're splattering us with cover fire which means they're inching up the hallways. We don't have much time.

I just keep thinking I wish I'd have had time to put some clothes on.

"As soon as the alarm went off, I realized what must have happened and I set this all into motion. I had hoped that you would have shot him while in the hangar as

●

"Wait, I—I don't understand…" Sylas says, holding his hand to the bullet hole in his chest. The blood flows around his fingers, it's coming so fast. Around us the bullets embed themselves in the walls, or ping off and spin wild.

"What is there to understand?" I ask, crouching lower as something buzzes past my head.

"I'm not him. Van Ryan, I mean."

"Then…then who *are* you?" he asks.

What the hell. "What the hell," I say with a sigh. As if on cue, the bullets stop flying. "Might as well tell you now."

"Sigma Three-Seven. Come out!" someone yells from back down the hall. That's the code.

These goons have been my extraction guys the whole time.

That makes the day a whole lot better.

"Gimme a second, willya?" I yell, my natural accent coming back into my voice. Sylas's eyes are so wide you could park a truck in them. The shock he's feeling makes it so that I don't think he's feeling the bullets in him. I point the pistol at him. With my other hand, I pull the

245

comcard out of my briefs. "It's actually hard to remember my name, do you believe it?" I laugh. "I've been trying to for the last ten minutes but for the life of me, I can't." I press the button on the card and a small red light starts to flash.

"Confirmed," a woman yells from behind me somewhere.

"Look," I say, "for what it's worth, I can see that you really did believe. That you honestly thought this revolution of yours was going to work out. If it means anything to you, this isn't a failure on your part. There was nothing you could have done that would have changed any of this. This was all—,"

"Come out!" the woman from before yells.

"Okay," I yell back over my shoulder. I sigh as I look into this guy, Sylas' face. I can see that he's only just now starting to put the whole thing together. "This was all in motion long before you ever met whoever this was to you," I say, gesturing to my own body. "As they say, it's possible to do everything correctly and still lose."

Sylas is shaking his head slow back and forth. He starts to cry. I can hear the team moving in closer.

"Come out!" someone yells. I can hear that they are closer than they were before. There's a clock on this thing.

"I said, give me a second!" I yell back. "When Olver opened himself up to try to buy this guy, Van Ryan, people saw an opportunity."

"What people?" Sylas whispers. I'm wondering how much blood could possibly be left in him.

"People," I say. "So, they came up with this plan. A long con. And they found me. Even I will admit I was a nothing, a zero, really. I had the skills they were looking for, though. So, fifteen surgeries later—which I'm told is a lot for this kind of thing, but they said they had to be sure—here I am."

"No," Sylas whispers.

I laugh to myself. "It's amazing how fast you wind up into someone for a lot of money. I was just having a bad luck streak, but there they were all of a sudden. All the debt paid off for just this one thing. One job and out. Not even that horrible, as jobs go. I mean, Olver isn't bad looking. But then I guess there was you," I say.

Someone over in the hallway says just loud enough I can hear them, "What's the extraction code word?"

They told me to expect that. That's the reason for the card. I flip it over and read it. "Bananas." I laugh.

"And the other one?" the guy yells.

I look at Sylas. I'm not supposed to say the second code word until the job is done. Technically it is—Olver is dead and his power is crippled. I didn't do it myself, but Sylas's revolution is handling all that as we speak. They don't know that a horde of drop ships, like wasps invading a beehive, have come plunging through the ocean to settle in the landing bays they've just fought so hard to win. They don't know that troops will empty out of those landing ships and gun down everyone still standing on their way to the capital building.

All I have to do is say the word and the team in the hallway will sweep in and take me to the ship I was promised which will take me back to orbit and then back to Earth where I can have my life back.

All I have to do is pull the trigger one more time, ending Sylas's life which is already spilling out around his fingers.

And that's when I remember it. Like something from a dream, it comes through a fog, materializing at the top of my mind.

I look into his eyes. He knows. "Aaron Murray," I say. His eyes close like a final bell. I pull the trigger and his forehead explodes.

"Parador," I say, standing up. I toss the pistol onto the table so there's no confusion.

They sweep in around the corner from the hallway. The red dots slide over me like a rain, like a bath. I put my hands up with my palms toward them.

"Final code?" One of the men asks as they finish sweeping the room.

There was one last word I was told to memorize. So important that they wouldn't even put it on a card. It's the one that tells them who I am and ends all of this.

"Pauper," I say. I feel my shoulders relax, tons of weight lifting from them in an instant. For a moment, I wonder how long I'll be in hospital while they put my real face back on.

I see the man nod. Then I see him bring his rifle up to his shoulder and the red light flares in my eyes for a second.

"Wha—?" I start to ask, then everything goes black.

# EPILOGUE

"One last item—we have word from Velarius Station," the young man says, closing the leather cover of his tablet.

"Oh? Good news, I trust?" the old man says, leaning back in his chair. Outside the glass, Los Angeles glows in cold neon rain.

"Very good, as a matter of fact. It seems the operative not only brought down the current regime, and executed the plan perfectly, allowing our operatives entrance, but he also uncovered a coup already underway, used it to his advantage, and eliminated *that* leader, as well. Our men now have control of the entire station."

The old man swished his cognac around in its snifter for a moment, sniffed it, then took a sip. His eyes closed as he savored the sweet sting of it on his tongue. "I see," he says. "And the operative?"

"Eliminated as per the plan," the young man says.

"Excellent," the old man says. "Loose ends are so untidy."

Outside the window, it begins to rain. The old man stands, straightens his coat, then walks to the elevator and is gone in moments. The young man picks up the snifter of cognac and drains the last of it in one gulp, then leaves as well.

www.ingramcontent.com/pod-product-compliance
Lightning Source LLC
Chambersburg PA
CBHW031213260626
47169CB00007B/2046